JOSEPH MALARA

The Guide to Christian Dating, Marriage, and Sex

The Guide to Christian Dating, Marriage, and Sex

Straight Talk about Christian Relationships

JOSEPH MALARA

The Guide to Christian Dating, Marriage and Sex

Straight Talk about Christian Relationships

Most Christians are clueless on how to date, when to date, why to date, who to date, and who to marry…

A MUST-READ if you are DATING or LOOKING to date, if you're ENGAGED, SEPARATED, DIVORCED, MARRIED, or

RE-MARRIED.

This Book is for YOU!

Contents edited by **Aimee Malara**

Cover design by **Aimee Malara**

Written by **Joseph Malara,** *Theologian*

For more information and to view videos concerning this book and other books, visit

www.JosephMalara.com

JOSEPH MALARA

Copyright © 2022, Joseph Malara

Revised Copyright © 2026 Joseph Malara

ISBN: 979-8-9859553-0-9

I have revised and updated this book, along with others, to ensure they remain current, clearer, and more comprehensive, offering better explanations and information for all readers. Each book is available worldwide online and can be viewed or purchased on my website. I also created a short video for each book I authored, explaining its contents. Please visit www.JosephMalara.com

I pray that God uses even these humble books He has allowed me to write to draw YOU closer to HIM.

Email me for more information or questions you may have, JosephMalara@yahoo.com

MALARA HAS ALSO WRITTEN:

1. The Bible on How to Box

2. Celebrity Sculptures & Hands of Stone, My Story

3. God's Clarity Through Poetry

4. God's Clarity Through Poetry 2

5. Digging Deeper into God's Truth Defines a Christian

6. **The Guide to Christian Dating, Marriage, and Sex**

7. IT'S ALL SUBJECT TO GOD'S WORD

8. Examine The End Times

9. Many Beliefs, But God

For each publication I authored, I created a short video explaining it. These books are available online or on my website. Please take a look.

www.JosephMalara.com

Contents

Contents

Acknowledgments

I need to openly and sincerely thank You, Father God, for allowing me a New Life in spite of my wretched self and shameful past. When I cried out to You, You did not end my life but gave me a New Heart and Eternal Life. Salvation in Christ is the greatest Gift of all. Although I was exceedingly wicked and foolish, You were there. You, Your Son, and Your Spirit have allowed me to experience sorrow and pain to Your Glory. Specifically, right now, through my mere books, You guide my words while using Yours. Books that can be used by You to help others to better understand Your corrections, Truths, provisions, and eternal love. There are others who are Yours too. They also seek Biblical guidance and counsel to apply to their own relationship with You and their relationships with others. God, You helped me to better understand, recognize, and obey Your Laws, Concepts, and Principles. You always had my back; my life is in Your Hands and always has been. You continued to love me, even when I hated myself. You gave me to Your Son; for that I will always be Eternally Grateful.

There are no words righteous enough, correct enough, and honorable enough or loving enough that could ever explain Your Charity and deep Love towards me. Even now, You bless me with the second greatest Gift of all…the greatest woman in the world, my wife. Thank you, my God and my Lord…thank you.

Introduction

Do YOU want *"straight talk"* as YOU search for a real <u>Christian Relationship?</u> Do you **understand how to accurately and thoroughly vet your next Christian date?** Are YOU confused about why your current relationship isn't **working?** Do YOU have a **great SEX life** with your spouse? When it comes to your marriage, are you both connecting with each other, or not communicating **at all?** YOU found the right Book! This book goes where other Christian writers won't… to the real truth of the matter.

I will use Biblical Truths and principles. I will expose and expand on what God's Word teaches concerning a relationship with Him and your date or spouse. This book includes chapters on that MOST important first date: knowing when to say NEXT! A chapter on what the RED FLAGS are to look out for concerning your current or future relationship.

Are YOU searching for someone who shares the same Biblical Truths as you do? Does he or she have the **same God of the Bible**? Do YOU want a Godly Relationship or not, one where you both grow closer to Jesus and each other, each day? All these topics and much more are addressed in this book!

Chapter 1

The Christian Dating Process

I have wanted to write such a book for many, many years. I have witnessed countless relationships with zero guidance and no moral blueprint for how to proceed or succeed. **When in a relationship or courting, if your conduct is not Biblical, your marriage won't be either.** This book goes where few, if any, Christian writers have ever dared to go. There are many reasons God allowed me to write this book. Ultimately, through Biblical relational mistakes, I learned from Him to recognize the right woman. When He saved me, I was always praying to Him for His wisdom and knowledge to lead to the right spouse, the one He wanted for me. He knew and knows my heart better than I do. I am not boasting, nor am I proud of having had countless relationships with women in my past. Although when I was lost and single, I was blind to Him. I was saved two weeks after my divorce. That marriage lasted fourteen years. I have had several life-altering "Christian" relationships over the past fourteen years. I will relate to those false Christian relationships to better help instruct and educate readers.

These were all Bible-learning relationships that led up to the Biblical marriage to my current and true Christian wife. What Satan meant for bad, God meant and/or allowed for Good. I suggest that, while reading this book, you use a yellow marker to highlight points of interest and keep your Bible nearby for reference. There is a blank page in the back of this book for NOTES. **When you find that *right* spouse, your heart will**

11

see this person with such contrast that it can only be compared between a *"Lightning Bug"* and a *"Bolt of lightning!"* This book will be your personal guide in doing just that.

Through constant study of God's Word, my eyes began to see what and who were truly the most important: God. His design for marriage is perfect and full of intimacy. This illustrates the relationship between Christ, Who is God, and His Church, which is His Believers, His Bride, His Children, His Elect. **Read this entire book, even if a chapter may not pertain to you. Biblical Truths are "one size fits all."** If you can take away one idea, one principle, one concept, one thought, just one new Biblical perception that may help you in your walk with Christ, this book would have accomplished its purpose. I prayed to God before writing this book and throughout its writing that it might help many. **Pray before reading it, that it may be a benefit to you.**

There is no money in writing Christian books. If I weren't a Christian, maybe I would be writing romance novels. I wrote this book because there is an obvious need for it. **As a Christian, many are clueless on how to date, when to date, why to date, and who to date.** Most Believers don't understand how to love each other once married or how to keep their marriage strong. God is The Great Awakening, His Principles and Concepts work. A Christian's life ultimately is for God's Glory, through Jesus the Christ. **A True Christian Marriage will showcase the love of Christ in both lives.** Let's start by understanding the human heart. Let's go to **Jeremiah 17:9 NKJV:** *"The heart is deceitful above all things, and* *desperately wicked; Who can know it?"* We read here that my heart and your heart are both wicked, desperately wicked. The only hope and true love in our hearts is Christ! Therein lies the sole reason **YOU ONLY WANT TO DATE AND MARRY A TRUE BELIEVER.**

This book will bring very important factors to the table, shining a bright light on why and how a Christian relationship and marriage should work. This book will include how and why one must continue to grow in Biblical Truths. This includes marital sex, oneness, and sincere love, all while placing Christ first. I will unpack what will build up a marriage, what will tear it down and destroy it, and how to save one. I will prove marriage is a gift from God. In marriage, your spouse must be placed second to God to be fully treasured.

I have been asked for my opinion on Godly Relationships by countless strangers on social media, previous readers of my other books, and Christian friends. Most people who are saved and lost wanted me to give them Biblical answers to their questions, which is why this book was written. My previous books did not dig deep enough into this crucial foundational covenant between a man and a woman. A real man doesn't *"love"* a million women; he loves one woman a million ways. I have written countless poems on and about relationships throughout my life, some of which I will include in this book. I have been writing creatively since I was 13 years old. My first published book was a poetry book entitled *"God's Clarity Through Poetry."* I wrote that book as an *unlearned Christian,* an Arminian *(a false doctrine that holds to free will in salvation), during God's early sanctification* in my life, back in

2006. This was before I had fully read the Bible and before God enabled me to fully recognize His doctrine of Election and His purpose in my life *(more on this later)*. When I try to explain God's Election to most people, at the beginning of their walk with Jesus, it is a slippery slope. ***Election in a nutshell means God Chose you before you chose Him.*** My last Poetry book is 100% Biblical and titled "God's Clarity Through Poetry 2," which focuses on Biblical relationships with deeper insight. I highly recommend you read that book as well.

If you are reading this book as a Christian, then you must want to do as God instructs. ***The right behavior follows the right belief.*** Keeping that in mind while you read will help you to fully grasp what God wants for you in a relationship. **This book will try to cover the subject of relationships, leading to a healthier marriage, and pinpoint those headed for disaster!** The marital bond is one set in place by God, and without Him, there is only confusion, pain, misunderstandings, and constant regrets. I was not really starting over in each new relationship, but learning from experience. As a Christian and after over a decade of dating the wrong women, I was able to learn from those experiences how to properly **VET** a real Christian date.

Let's go to **Genesis 2:18-24 NASB** *(18) Then the Lord God said, "It is not good for the man to be alone; I will make him a helper suitable for him." (19) And out of the ground the Lord God formed every animal of the field and every bird of the sky, and brought them to the man to see what he would call them; and whatever the man called a living creature, that was its name. (20) The man gave names to all the livestock, and to the birds of the sky, and to every animal of the field, but for*

14

Adam there was not found a helper suitable for him. (21) So the Lord God caused a deep sleep to fall upon the man, and he slept; then He took one of his ribs and closed up the flesh at that place. (22) And the Lord God fashioned into a woman the rib which He had taken from the man, and brought her to the man. (23) Then the man said "At last this is bone of my bones, And flesh of my flesh; She shall be called 'woman,' Because she was taken out of man." (24) For this reason a man shall leave his father and his mother, and be joined to his wife; and they shall become one flesh.

Let's unpack these verses. This is the first time in the Bible where God said, "It is NOT good" for man to be alone. This is the account of the first marriage. We see that Adam named everything, including all the animals, which were male and female. We see that God, in His Infinite Wisdom and Judgment, did not want man to be alone or without a helper. Let's stop here and explain what God meant by *"helper."* This means a married man's wife would prepare food, clothing, and other personal needs for her husband. She would be available for companionship and sexual relations (*we will address this later*). She must take care of any children, including their education. We cannot trust today's public educational systems, which will brainwash children with anti-biblical views along with a Godless liberal agenda. Home schooling may be the only real option. Christian parents must profess and explain Biblical Truths to their children, including the Biblical Gospel.

Regarding work for the wife outside the home, I do not suggest that as an option. If the husband is self-employed, she should help him with his business as a partner. Remembering each business has a president, or manager, head person, or leader, such will and must always be the man. **The woman is his helper, not the other way around.** That reversal of leadership has shattered countless families. There are reasons God made this "Role Call," and it is His Way for us to do life. A woman was taken out of a man, not out of his head to top him, not out of his feet to be stepped on, but out of his side to be protected by him; **from his side to be his helpmate** and near his heart to be loved by him.

This does not make one spiritually superior to the other. We are all equal in Christ, but just as Generals are over Sergeants or a Sergeant over a Private or a Captain over his ship, man is over his wife. God has given "Headship" for man to be over his wife and his family *(if they have a family)*. The verses in Genesis chapter 2 also illuminate how God created woman and explain that a man and woman, while in marriage, are one flesh. This is to say no longer two but one. This is where only God's math works. If two become one, then there should be no conflict, no division, no confusion, no separation, for one cannot be divided again. **They are *"One in Christ"* and of the same purpose, to serve God.** Their goals are the same: to raise Godly Children, love each other, and grow in all of God's Truths. They are to tell others of The Gospel of Jesus, plant seeds of Truth, feed the Sheep *(God's Children)*, cultivate other Disciples, and be an example of the Living Word *(Christ)*.

Let's take a look at **Genesis 3:16-17 NASB** (16) *To the woman He (God) said, "I will greatly multiply your pain in childbirth, in pain you shall deliver children; yet your desire will be for your husband, and he shall rule over you." (17) Then to*

16

Adam He said, "Because you have listened to the voice of your wife, and have eaten from the tree about which I commanded you, saying, 'You shall not eat from it'; Cursed is the ground because of you; With hard labor you shall eat from it All the days of your life. Let's unpack these two verses. First, we see the aftereffects of Eve eating the forbidden fruit. Satan went to the weaker vessel, Eve. She ate the fruit and gave it to Adam, her husband, and he did the same. This was how sin entered the world. We see here that God spoke to them both and laid out the law, which is still in effect today. **God said to Eve *(meaning all women)*, " Your desire will be for your husband, and he will rule over you.** This is quoting God in the above verse, Genesis 3:16. If any woman takes issue with this statement, **as to not like it, their issue is not with their husband but with God.** This is one of today's biggest rebellious issues due to the evil Godless "Feminist Movement." Quoting Helen Andelin (Founder of the Fascinating Womanhood Movement), *"To awaken chivalry, we must return to femininity. We must stop doing the masculine things and become the gentle, tender, dependent women we were designed to be."*

What did God say to Adam? God lectured Adam for listening to his wife! **Since Adam was the Captain of his ship, Adam was at fault.** Marriage is the strongest of bonds when we let God take control by fully obeying His Word. This must be completely understood before marriage. **This means the man will rule over his wife. The man is the leader, and the woman must follow his lead.** This distinction must be obeyed, agreed to, honored, and followed. A marriage where the woman takes charge, disobeying this Godly principle, is and would be disastrous. This is painfully obvious in today's society. Let's

17

turn to **Titus 2:4-5 ESV** *(4) and (older woman) so train the young women to love their husbands and children, (5) to be self-controlled, pure, working at home, kind, and submissive to their own husbands, that the word of God may not be reviled.* Throughout Scripture, God was very clear as to who must lead. God was also very clear about a woman's role in her life.

Let's take a look at **Ecclesiastes 4:9-12 KJV** *Two are better than one; because they have a good reward for their labor. For if they fall, the one will lift up his companion: but woe to him that is alone when he falleth; for he hath not another to help him up. Again, if two lie together, then they have heat: but how can one be warm alone? And if one prevail against him, two shall withstand him; and a threefold cord is not quickly broken.* Here we see that two working together yields more rewards, double the workload, double the benefits. If one falls down, the other is there to help them up. This has more meaning than meets the eye. In life, we all fall. When one does, the other can either step on his or her fingers, making the fall much worse, or show mercy by helping him or her up. Many times, there's a life-altering moment or a relationship-ending moment. If one doesn't run to God first, seeking His Advice using His Wisdom and His Word, it won't end well. ***Do NOT seek the advice of some lost friend, family member, or psychologist.***

These verses go on to say two can stay warm together; this shows intimacy, being alone does not. If one prevails against him or her, it means an adversary comes against one of the two. You both will have each other, which is two against one, overpowering the one. **This threefold or three-strand cord is "God's Knot," symbolizing the joining of one man, one** woman, and God into a marriage relationship. This unity can only be accomplished by placing God in the center of your marriage, having a "God Centered Marriage." God must be the *"Go Between Person,"* the One Who not only oversees your marriage but is in control of it. This is only possible through constant daily prayer, including studying God's Word together. **If you merely study to remember, you will forget. When you study to *learn* God's Word, you will remember.** Then apply His Guidelines, His Precepts, His Principles, His Values, His Morals, and His Boundaries, including His Grace, into your own marriage, because that's what's required.

The driving force behind this book is the essence of why Christian Relationships work and why some do not work. I would be foolish not to unpack what a description of a "Christian" relationship truly is or should be. **This type of relationship is foreign to the world; foreign to the mindset of those who do not know and live for Jesus.** It is foreign to those who are not themselves Born Again by God. However, to those who are His, this book will be a breath of fresh air, a cool breeze of God's Truth, a tall glass of ice water on a hot sunny day. Let me elaborate: when looking for a date while claiming to be a Christian, it is very different from what it was like before a person's heart was converted by God.

Salvation is not merely making a good person better, it's not making a sick person well, and it's not only the changing of one's mind. Salvation is GOD making a DEAD PERSON ALIVE IN CHRIST. Salvation by God completely transforms and supplies one with a new heart in Christ. Let's look at 2 **Corinthians 5:17 NKJV** *Therefore, if anyone is in*

Christ, he is a new creation; old things have passed away; behold all things have become new. This verse is saying that when one is Born Again by God they are NOT the same person at all. **Their desires change; there is a turning point towards God. The things they wanted to do before becoming Saved are the things they would rather not do again.** Their heart lives for the Glory of God. God gives His Children the power over sin as well as the forgiveness of it. This type of person is not sinless, but they sin less. They repent of their sins, seeking to cease them with God's help. **Your relationship with Christ will affect every other relationship you will have for the rest of your life, if you are a REAL CHRISTIAN.** Your Salvation brings unspeakable joy and a noticeable passion for God that cannot be hidden. **We live to give God Glory; this is the true passion of one Saved by God.** Here is an eye-opening quote from Martyn Lloyd Jones, a Protestant Minister & Medical Dr.: *"If you do not desire to be Holy, then you have NO right to think that you are a Christian."*

A Christian is a person who craves the Truths of God's Word, loves to study His Word, and tells others about Jesus. They love correction, rebuke, and instruction from someone using God's Word. **Believers realize they cannot grow beyond their ability to receive correction.** This points to **2 Timothy 3:16 KJV** *All scripture is given by inspiration of God, and is profitable for doctrine, for reproof, for **correction**, for instruction in righteousness.* When we use God's Word, this verse says many things that **false believers hate** and will certainly go against. **The world does not want correction but appeasement concerning their false ways of thinking.**

Let's look at **Proverbs 9:8 NIV** *Do not rebuke mockers, or they will hate you; rebuke the wise, and they will love you.* The world does not want to use the Bible for reproof; they think the Bible is not written nor inspired by God, but by man. The world wants no instruction towards their behavior or evil ways. **The world's lost people want your approval and compliance for their endless sins and inaccuracies.** The lost world, the unregenerate heart, is unconcerned about such things as sin. This one verse, 2 Timothy 3:16, separates the Sheep *(God's Elect)* from the goats *(Satan's children, those of the world).* Don't date a goat. Let's look at **Mark 3:25 NASB:** *If a house is divided against itself, that house will not be able to stand.* **This is why a Christian must "VET"** *(totally examine)* **other "Christians" most thoroughly. You will soon find out that this is the single most important element concerning a God-centered relationship.** Here is a verse that may help you understand how true Christians live. Let's turn to **2 Timothy 3:12 ESV:** *Indeed, all who desire to live a Godly life in Christ Jesus will be persecuted.* Let's unpack this verse from the Apostle Paul. It clearly states that you will lose everyone you love. Now, the one who is truly Saved must ask themselves, *"Who do I desire most?"* **Concerning Biblical Salvation, our contribution is to do what Lazarus did from his Tomb; respond when God Calls.** The only thing we contribute to our own Salvation is OUR sin. *In this book, I will purposely convey the same important facts and issues in several different ways to better drive home their significance. Some things must be repeated several times to stress importance.*

Real Christians are not popular, but despised. Genuine converted Believers have a backbone. They have intestinal fortitude when confronted with false truths, false teachers, and false doctrines. Therefore, when a Real Christian man is looking for a Real Christian woman to marry, she fits this description as well. She will wait to get married before having sex. She would be the one to fight for God's Word. She will show endless devotion to her husband even in the face of adversity. She will want to serve and love her man endlessly. She will want to be submissive; therefore, in obedience to her husband. She will always want to pray with and for her husband and others. She will long to read and study God's Word with her husband as well. Quoting Martha Peace (Woman's Bible Teacher, Author), *"A wife should realize that being submissive is a FRUIT of her Salvation."* Again, such a Biblical belief is foreign to this fallen world. It is the right way of life for all True Believers. **True Believers Glorify God by loving Him enough to obey Him.** Here is a poem, "Helpmate," from my second poetry book, entitled "God's Clarity Through Poetry 2." Give it a read.

SO, THEY ARE NO LONGER TWO, BUT ONE FLESH. THEREFORE, WHAT GOD HAS JOINED TOGETHER, NO PERSON IS TO SEPARATE."

MATTHEW 19:6

Helpmate

When a man fails with his endeavors, business, or finances…guess who his helper is? When a man awakes with a merry heart and that feeling is soon altered, his spirit broken apart…guess who his helper is?

When a man full of ambition fails at his mission…guess who his helper is? When a man's home is full of clutter, chaos, and disarray with no peace each day…guess who his helper is?

A house divided cannot stand, and won't, if not led by the man...we each have a Godly role and if we go against God's Word...it will surely take its toll...

When a man climbing the wall of life...needs his wife...for love, intimacy, affection, conversation, provision, help...and she does not care, she's not there...yes, he will fall...but guess who pushes him off that wall...his helper...

But, when there's a marriage that works, there's a helpmate ready and willing to do all she can to assist her man...not sabotage him, if and when she can...she is his real-time helper, not a hurter and never, ever a liar, cheat, or deserter...

She places his wants and needs well above her own...promoting a happy home...regardless of any circumstance or any incident, or state of affairs...she's always there for him and for him always cares...

She is under the legitimate authority of her husband, and he is under the legitimate authority of Christ...without this order there's only disorder...

Behind every respectable man of God...is a great and noble woman of God...Helpmates are groomed by God's Word and fear God and are supporters of their husband's needs...

and men of God respect their wives with all their hearts and would die to protect and support their helpmates' well-being...

As Christ loved His Church and died for it...so few of this description fit...

it is a sin...and it is impossible...unless Born Again...to even understand and to this concept give in...

Genesis 2:18 KJV *And the Lord God said, It is not good that the man should be alone; I will make him an help meet for him.*

      True Christians are always going through a period of sanctification *(being more Christ-like through Biblical correction daily),* and they want little to do with sinning against God. **The sins that pleased them before Jesus came into their hearts, they soon detest.** They grow to hate the sin they once loved. They grow each day closer to love the Righteousness they once ignored. **They have a newfound burden for others' lost souls and do something about it. They often pray for the lost souls.** They want to please God more and NOT themselves.

Is this a reality in YOUR life? The world has become a foreign place to them. Let's go to **James 4:4 ESV** *You adulterous people! Do you not know that friendship with the world is enmity with God? Therefore, whoever wishes to be a friend of the world makes himself an enemy of God.* Let's unpack this verse. It's saying that if God's Love is in you, you will be hated by the world because such is the enemy of God. You will also grow to hate the world yourself.

If you want to follow Jesus, expect to be treated like Jesus; hated! Let's unpack **John 10:27 NKJV** *My sheep hear My voice, and I know them, and they follow Me.* Here, we must all recognize that Jesus is saying three things: His Sheep (His Elect) hear His Voice, not the world's. He also says they follow Him, as in obey Him. He also adds <u>He Knows Them.</u> We must now look at **Matthew 7:23 NKJV** *And then I will declare to them, 'I never knew you; depart from Me, you who practice lawlessness!'* Jesus is speaking here concerning those He throws into Hell on Judgment Day. We should notice that Jesus says here, *"He never knew them."* What this means is that they are NOT His Elect, NOT His. This book will expose the many signs that help pinpoint those who are His and those who are NOT His. Let's look at **Matthew 7:22 NKJV** *Many will say to Me in that day, 'Lord, Lord, have we not prophesied in Your name, cast out demons in Your name, and done many wonders in Your name?'* Here, we see people who say they KNOW Jesus. They profess to be His Children. They say Lord, Lord as to confirm that they are genuinely surprised *Jesus doesn't know them; in the same way as He Knows His Elect.* The Elect are those who live for Jesus and obey His Commandments; they love Him and are loved by Him.

26

It's now **John 14:15 NJKV** *"If you love Me, keep My Commandments."* Jesus is talking to those who love Him and trust Him. These are His True Followers who have an intimate relationship with Him.

If you still love the old life you had before or the same un-Godly friends, family, and/or material things, you may not be Born Again, but just think you are. That was me for decades…but God… If you were to become more Christ-like, you would be hated; remember, they crucified Jesus. The world loved Barabbas *(a well-known criminal & murderer); they set him free and killed Jesus, who was without any sin* and was God incarnate. They will do the same to you, it's Matthew 10:22 NASB, *and you will be hated by all because of My name (Jesus), but it is the one who has endured to the end who will be saved.* <u>You should discuss this verse and many others in this book on your first date. It's important that you scrutinize each other correctly, honestly, and Biblically.</u> **It's vitally important that as a Christian, you do not waste ANY time dating fake Christians!** I wasted close to fourteen years doing this, frivolous years; thus, this book. Hopefully, you will not make the same mistakes I have after reading this book; I pray. **Judge a man or woman by the closeness he or she has with the God of the Bible.** Search him or her to examine and cross-examine, which will reveal his or her inner thoughts and inner self. If these thoughts are mostly about him or her, that's who his or her "god" is. Never be afraid to ask probing questions. Ask: If married, would you like children? If so, how many? **Remember, you are ultimately looking for Mr. or Miss Right, not Mr. or Miss right now!**

Let's look at **2 Corinthians 6:14 NKJV** *Do not be unequally yoked together with unbelievers. For what fellowship has righteousness with lawlessness? And what communion has light with darkness?* Here it is plain to see that you will have nothing in common with those who love the world. You will have a considerable amount in common with those who belong to God. **If you date because of lust, it will end very badly.** If you date someone just because you like them, it will end badly. If you date someone because you think you can love them, it will end very badly. **If you are simply physically attracted to the other person, even if they are not Born Again, it will end very badly.** There comes a time when the love of God is all you want. A person must see that God-like love in their date before moving on. When your companion wants the old life, things get really bad, really soon. **Examine, observe, and evaluate! Ask countless questions.** Enroll in Christian Pre-Marital courses. I have been to a few after the first one, and I was asked to teach the class. I declined but was humbly honored. That first course revealed to me that the woman I thought I wanted was not what God wanted for me. In fact, she was the worst person for me! My poems in this book will reveal much. The second time, several years later, I went through a different Christian Pre-Marital course. This time, that course helped me realize that the woman I had chosen then turned out to be the "Jezebel" type.

I recommend following this advice when looking for that special someone to marry. **First, you must confirm their Christian Faith is REAL.** Secondly, find someone who knows ALL of your flaws *(because you must be honest)* and recognizes ALL of your mistakes, weaknesses, and still thinks you're completely amazing! God has allowed me to go through much,

28

so I may be experienced enough, able, and qualified to write this book. I have read many books written by other authors on relationships and marriage. Unfortunately, most writers only had one relationship! A particular writer married his high school sweetheart, so he had no life experience to draw on. Life is not always that simple, nor does it work out that way for us all.

A wounded Christian will search the Scriptures as one seeks for gold. God cannot greatly use anyone until that person is deeply hurt by HIM. There is no way one could write such a book as this using other people's experiences. A person must know and feel real hurt to fully understand how God changes their heart. God also changes a person's preferences, so we want to place Him first in all things. **The Bible was written to God's Children. It is not just for <u>information but for transformation</u>.** It is the *Living Word,* a living book, a Spiritual book. You will see new things each time you read and study it. No one can ever finish reading The Bible. **The Bible is Supernatural, not superficial; it is ALL God-breathed and inerrant. The more God is on your mind, the more He is in your heart.** Therefore, the more you are able, confident, equipped, and open to tell others the *Good News* of Jesus. **The Christian must realize that he or she was made by God and for God, and only until he or she understands this will his or her life make any sense.**

What's most important while writing or reading such a book as this is to know we are among God's Elect. Let's read **1 John 5:13 NASB:** *These things I have written to you who believe in the name of the Son of God, so that you may **know** that you have eternal life.* There is no guessing game concerning

29

God's Children. They KNOW they belong to Jesus, because of the words that are written in Scripture. These words are loud and clear to those who have ears to hear. His Words can also be damning, saying, *"Get Right with God!"* The path God has put me on as I walk through my sanctification has equipped me to write such a book. I had real-life experiences, and through them, I learned true Biblical discernment. This came from many years of constant Bible studies. Hopefully, this book will guide others facing similar circumstances and help them avoid the same pitfalls. I also felt the real deep pain. Let's read **Hebrews 12:6-8 NASB** *(6) For whom the Lord loves He disciplines, And He punishes every son whom He accepts." (7) It is for discipline that you endure; God deals with you as with sons; for what son is there whom his father does not discipline? (8) But if you are without discipline, of which all have become partakers, then you are illegitimate children and not sons.* The writer of Hebrews teaches that God disciplines those He calls His own. **When a person is used by God, they will be brought to their knees; this shows that He is all they need.**

The ones who are His go through the loss of friends and family, the loss of those closest to them. If you don't go through a separation between you and this world, you are not a true son or daughter of God, but an illegitimate one. **I have been through great separation with those who love the world and with those I truly love.** I have also been fooled by many women into believing their story of Salvation was real, simply based on what they said. That is not always a good indication of salvation, but God's Fruits and Biblical Truths are. Salvation is never based solely on something someone says, does, or doesn't do. **God's love for His Children takes them out of the world.**

30

Therefore, he or she is ostracized from those they love. Jesus was hated, and His Children will be as well. **God's love is not a pampering love but a perfecting love, based on mercy, not merit.**

Let's examine **Romans 8:28 NASB** *And we know that God causes all things to work together for good to those who love God, to those who are called according to His purpose.* Here we see that God is Sovereign. He alone allows things or directs things towards His Will, not ours. This verse is focused on His calling. Those "Called" are His Elect, and we are Called for His Purpose, not ours. The purpose once saved is to please Him, glorify Him, and do His will, which is found only in His Word. Our lives become all about Him, not us.

If you're at a family get-together and no one wants to speak of God or mention what God is doing in their lives, it's because they are Godless. They won't even give thanks (grace) for the food! You should not be surprised or baffled by this; they are of the world. **Those who live for themselves rather than for Christ are NOT His.** People of the world, including so-called "Christians," often get upset when you teach them what is in the Bible rather than what they presume is in it. God's Children love Biblical Correction and apply it to their lives. Quoting Martin Luther (Theologian, Reformer), *"Show me where a man spends his time and his money, and I'll show you his god."* I would concur, Brother Martin!

The People who offend you with God's Truths do not hate you. The people who comfort you with worldly lies hate you. If you prefer a comfortable lie over an offensive Biblical

Truth, you hate yourself and want to remain lost and uninformed. Here is a quote from R.C. Sproul (Reformed Theologian & Pastor) that clearly identifies how our lives as true Believers should be. *"We do not segment our lives, giving some time to God, some to our business, or schooling, while keeping parts to ourselves. The idea is to live all of our lives in the presence of God, under the authority of God, and for the honor and glory of God. That is what the Christian life is all about."* **We can clearly comprehend from this quote how few true Christians there really are.**

Chapter 2

Think Red Flag

When you are on a date, you MUST learn when to say "NEXT!" Start with the premise that NO ONE IS GOOD, not one. This points to **Romans 3:10-12 KJV** *(10) As it is written, There is none righteous, no, not one:(11) There is none that understandeth, there is none that seeketh after God. (12) They are all gone out of the way, they are together become unprofitable; there is none that doeth good, no, not one.* This Truth is in both the Old Testament and the New Testament. **The only good in anyone is Christ. Remember this: there are three types of believers: un-believers, Believers, and make-believers. YOU should make certain that you date and marry a REAL Believer.**

You're not looking for some "character", but someone with character and with integrity. Let's unpack the above three verses. It's clear that no one is good. What if you say, "If I compare myself with Hitler, am I not better?" Clearly, no one is good; we are all wicked from birth. This Truth is one not understood by the lost world. There was only one Who was Good, and He died for those His Father gave Him. **Jesus is our Role Model.** In verse eleven, it says clearly that no one seeks God. **This is why He does ALL the seeking, not us**! Before He opens our eyes, we seek a false jesus, one of our own making. If you are found by Him, there will be fruit. This book will help you and others disclose such "fruit" moving forward. **We should never take anyone's word for it when he or she says, "I'm Saved!"**

When you have completed reading this book, you shouldn't be fooled again and again, and again, like I was.

In my relationships, **I have forgiven many so-called "christian women" (note small c) by giving them a second chance, third chance,** and so on. If the woman you are dating *(or the man you are dating) lies to you and you forgive him or her, yet you find him or her lying again,* think BIG Red Flag. **The lies could be little things, but if he or she would lie to you about little issues, why not BIG issues?** You should think Red Flag. If, while you are dating and in a relationship, and he or she looks at another woman or man, think Red Flag. When you notice your potential spouse places you **after** his/her family and friends, you must ask him or her, "Will that remain that way after marriage?" If this is the case, think Big Red Flag.

There should be NO communication between ex-wives or ex-husbands, unless minor children are involved. **Let's say you're serious with each other and find he or she is still communicating with an ex; think BIG Red Flag.** If you're a woman and your date does NOT open all your doors for you *(car, restaurant, house),* he has no manners; think Big Red Flag. If your man doesn't walk on the curb side while walking on a street, think Red Flag. If the one you want to date expresses any anger issues in **any capacity** or a temper at ANY time, there is no self-control; think BIG Red Flag. Let's read **Galatians 5:22-23 NASB** *(22) the fruit of the Spirit is love, joy, peace, patience, kindness, goodness, faithfulness, (23) gentleness,* **self-control***; against such things there is no law.* You can try to match your date to the fruits of the Spirit. How does he or she compare?

If you are ready to ask for her hand in marriage *(after asking her dad, of course)* and the road seems clear, then he or she wants to have sex; think <u>BIG Red Flag</u>. We know there will be heavy kissing and touching, which may be unavoidable, but sex can and must be avoided. You will not regret holding back until marriage, but if you have sex, you will regret having it before marriage; trust God. In most cases, once there is sex, everything changes. **They live for the sex; it becomes a drug they can't stop.** They soon forget that the love for God must come before the love of the flesh. **Sex is ONLY for marriage. This is the single most important thing that will ruin your testimony and relationship.** You will lose self-respect knowing you are sinning against a Holy and Righteous God. Your God.

You should know that having sex out of marriage is belittling the reason Jesus died for you; such is sin. Read now **Hebrews 13:4 NASB** *Marriage is to be held in honor among all, and the marriage bed is to be undefiled; for God will judge the sexually immoral and adulterers.* There comes a point in each serious relationship where this choice is out in the open. It's on the table, open to discussion and application. Don't do it. **Many Christians may not enjoy discipline, but they all enjoy the results.**

The man usually initiates a move towards having sex with his girlfriend or a woman friend. If the woman allows that and welcomes this act in place of smacking that man's face, that relationship is headed for a fall. **The woman must nip that request of his in the bud.** Her response will show her true colors. If she indulges in sex with her boyfriend or "some male friend," she will also have had sex with "other male friends." This is most likely their pattern. Now, if the woman stops her male friend from this sexual act, she is worth waiting for. Some people think that if you go out to dinner with a man, the woman owes him something. That's a lie from the pit of Hell. There are no such rewards at bargain prices. A man must marry a woman to have that privilege.

If the woman you are dating won't have sex with you regardless of your wicked persistence, she's a keeper. What about you? What does this say about you? She has expressed that she is Christ-like, and you have shown yourself unworthy of her. This shows that she loves God more, which is the correct response. At this point, you found out she is for real. You also found out what your weakness is; so, has she. **If, as a man, you try again and again after you have already been told by her, "NO," you are not worth her time.** The man should withdraw from that relationship. **This type of man is not looking for a wife, but a plaything. This exposes that person's true intention.**

The woman should end the relationship with such a persistent man; that's a <u>Big Red Flag</u>. Therefore, as a woman who tells her boyfriend or male friend, she will NOT have sex until marriage, yet he keeps trying, then you must run from him and think <u>BIG Red Flag</u>. He is NOT worth your love and cannot be trusted unless he will wait respectfully until after marriage. Let's look at **1 Corinthians 6:18 NLT** *Run from sexual sin! No other sin so clearly affects the body as this one does. For sexual immorality is a sin against your own body.* Concerning this sin, God tells us clearly what to do: **RUN** from it!

Now, let's flip this around. Let's say the woman initiates sex from you, the man, and you go for it. You are both now in a heated sexual relationship, which is against God. The man is always more sexually aggressive by nature because he simply has more testosterone than women. This aggression must be met with a harsh "NO" from your date. **There should be no excuses for having sex.** If she initiates sex from you, think Red Flag. If you allow her to enter into a sexual relationship with you, and she initiates it, why would you want her? **She is expressing that you are more important to her than God is.**

This is difficult here. I have had relationships where I was strong, and others where I was weak. Although my body said, yes, yes, yes, my Spirit said NO! Then, such women *(this happened on more than one occasion)* soon realized I would not do what they requested and no longer wanted to date me. They were deeply hurt; some expressions were *"I have never been turned down before."* Such an attitude shows they were not placing God first. This was what I needed to be exposed to. Therefore, they did me a favor by making their expectations clear. **There were other times I was not strong, nor were the women I dated, and such relationships always failed. I failed God many times.**

Let's refer to **Romans 7:19-20 NASB** *(19) For the good that I want, I do not do, but I practice the very evil that I do not want. (20) But if I do the very thing I do not want, I am no longer the one doing it, but sin that dwells in me.* Here, we read the Apostle Paul expressing the sin in us. As Believers, we do still sin. On the first date and beyond, in any relationship, do NOT lie to your date; be truthful. It's better to be slapped in the face with truth than kissed on the lips with a lie. **You don't get to pick when to tell the truth; the truth is beyond that.** You must both ask many questions, thus this book. You both should answer each question with kindness and complete honesty. Therefore, from day one in the dating stage, you both must promise to NOT have sex until married, period. Be honest in revealing who you truly are. **My failures were painful yet insightful; again, thus this book.** I truly feel that the woman MUST be stronger here. She is in full control of having sex or not having sex. It seems single men always want sex, and without a strong God-fearing woman, there's only failure knocking at the door. Regardless, both are and must be personally accountable to God for their actions; there is a price to pay. Let's look at **Proverbs 1:7 KJV** *The fear of the Lord is the beginning of knowledge: but fools despise wisdom and instruction.* If the date you are vetting does not fear the Lord, RUN! You are dealing with a lost fool. Remember, when vetting a date, **you are not there to change them.** We are to plant seeds of truth and move on. **You are searching for someone who is already genuinely saved; don't be bamboozled.**

You cannot save anyone. Read now **John 6:44 NASB** *No one can come to Me unless the Father who sent Me draws him; and I will raise him up on the last day.* Jesus is explaining Salvation clearly. It is all God, who does the choosing concerning Salvation, not any man. *Let's be very clear on this: our Soteriology must line up with God's Word.* This is evident throughout the whole Bible. **There is no such thing as free will concerning one's Salvation. That is a humanistic and pagan view of a Biblical and Spiritual concept.** Man's free will is imprisoned by sin. We have the free will to sin, which cannot overrule a Sovereign God. Let's look at **Galatians 2:20 NASB** *I have been crucified with Christ; and it is no longer I who live, but Christ lives in me; and the life which I now live in the flesh I live by faith in the Son of God, who loved me and gave Himself up for me.* We plainly see here that the Apostle Paul was indwelled as all Believers are with The Holy Spirit. This addition was NOT a choice Paul made, but a choice made for him on his behalf by God; such is Grace. **It is each Christian's duty to believe and to teach what the Bible teaches, not what you or I want to teach; again, don't be bamboozled!**

When God is not prominent in your life and/or your date's life, that weakness is the downfall. God will not be mocked. **You should think of "Who" you know, to help you say NO.** The "Christian" relationships that have sex before marriage don't work out so well. **We should love God enough to say "NO" to premarital sex.** God does not bless any unblessed behavior. If you are a man and she wants to have sex, she is not the right woman, <u>think Red Flag</u>. That goes both ways! Sex must be "ON HOLD" until Marriage, period! If you're the woman and he needs sex from you, get married first. If you're the man and she needs sex from you, get married first. **This is the moment of truth. Will you break up over such, or wait, or give in?** The Christian who wants to be right with God has only two answers: break up or wait. There are countless couples who get married at City Hall after obtaining a marriage license at their local County Clerk's Office; both must apply at the same time. It's that simple. The couple should read this book twice, pray, and then act on what they read. If, after reading this book, you find you are in a failing relationship, break it off! Do not waste his or her time. **Again, Christian dating is not for**

anything else but Marriage for the True Believer. It is better to wait than to settle. You should see yourself running a race to God's Kingdom. Look next to you; there's your future spouse, running the same race.

If you are so close to getting married and still have trust issues with him or her, think Red Flag. If you're not welcome to look at each other's cell phones *(at any time)* and don't know each other's passwords, think Red Flag. If either one is hiding their cell phone or changes their password, think Red Flag. When you're seriously courting, and you're not allowed to look in his wallet or her purse, think Red Flag. If the one you want as your spouse has secrets he or she won't tell you, think Red Flag. If either of you disrespects their family in front of the other, it's a sign of what your future with them might look like; think Red Flag. If a potential husband or wife wants you to learn to accept their relatives or friends' homosexual lifestyle, or sinful lifestyle, as to tolerate it, think Red Flag. If your man or woman belittles others or laughs at sin, think Red Flag. If a possible spouse relies on drugs, smoking, or alcohol to relieve stress or has such a habit, think Red Flag. **If your possible spouse takes any sin lightly, think Red Flag.** If your potential spouse speaks ill of others behind their back, one day they will do the same to you; think Red Flag. If your date does not have a real burden for lost souls, think Red Flag! If your date avoids or keeps you from reading together God's Word after you asked him or her to do so, think Big Red Flag! **Whatever or whoever keeps YOU from your Bible is an enemy of God. However harmless he or she may appear, RUN!**

If your date does not FEAR GOD, think BIG Red Flag! If you are trying to obey God, and he or she *makes it more difficult* so you don't, think Red Flag. If he or she is an embarrassment to you at any time, think Red Flag. **If he or she curses, think BIG Red Flag.** *Profanities are strong, Godless expressions from a weak Godless mind.* **If you heard him or her taking the Lord's name in vain, think BIG Red Flag.** If your potential spouse does not glorify God in their actions and words, think Red Flag. If your date is trying to hide you from their family, think Red Flag. If your date buys into false rumors about you, think Red Flag. **If he or she goes through a day without praying with you, or eats any meals without even saying "grace" (thanking God), think BIG Red Flag.** If your date is not sold out for Jesus, think Red Flag. **The above truths were gained through much experience and were very, very costly to me to learn firsthand. The knowledge you gain here in this book is what I needed to know over a decade ago!** God is good. Remember, many men and women are "Christian" in name only. Quoting Charles Spurgeon, known as the "Prince of Preachers," who preached during the 1800's, said, *"Not to pray because you do not feel fit to pray is like saying, I will not take medicine because I am too ill."* **Prayer brings us closer to God and changes our hearts to want what He wants for us. Stop reading for a moment now and pray that this book is a Godsend to your life.** ↑

I pray God helps you through whatever you may be going through concerning your relationship. In the past, I didn't know or even care to understand the information on these pages. I consistently entered into bad relationships with women. This **"Think Red Flag"** chapter was written to further explain and expose the three types of believers: non-believers, Believers, and make-believers. **We should understand that believing God is not the same as believing in God.** It may be difficult to end a relationship with the person you are courting; that is understandable. **If you continue to ignore the Red Flags, you will reap what you sow. Don't walk away from that relationship, run!** I have broken my own heart and those of others to do the right thing by God's standards, not the world's. I have also had my heart broken many times by others, but God did have a real plan. Let's refer to **Psalm 37:23 NASB** *The steps of a man are established by the Lord, And He delights in his way.* **When there are obvious <u>RED FLAGS,</u> do not ignore them; the time to run is before you get married.** When you run head-first into these RED FLAGS, what YOU should be thinking is…**NEXT!** If Jesus is not everything in your date's life, He is nothing. **Even ONE RED FLAG is enough to say, NEXT!** God willing…

Now, if you are already married, running is NOT an option. Working through difficulties is your option, and YOU must LOVE your spouse. **This is a Command from God.** This points to **John 13:34 NASB** *I am giving you a new commandment, that you love one another; just as I have loved you, that you also love one another.* Jesus here is commanding you to love. He says it two times, just in case you missed it the first time. When I hear foolish people say, *"I don't love her or him any longer,"* it's repulsive. God does command you to love; love her, love him; Period. This is the one YOU chose to marry. **Let me make this clear: Either Christ is the Lord of ALL in your life, or He is not Lord at all in your life.**

All the questions in this book directed towards a person's date or your ongoing relationship are not here as a mere list to check off yes or no √. **They are included in this book to be perceived as the correct way of life for the truly converted Believer. They are here to better expose the true intents of one's heart concerning Christ.**

Chapter 3

The Three "L's"

There are **three "L's"** I will refer to; **all three must be present for a relationship to work.** These are three truths that must complement each other in harmony and be evident in a relationship for it to succeed. First, "LIKE" means when you like someone, you are honestly kind to them. You sincerely want to help this person in their life. It's a heartfelt feeling. **Biblically, from the Greek word (Philia), it's a friendly love between equals.** You like him or her in spite of their flaws. You have great respect for this person. You like him or her regardless of their appearance, regardless of any other attributes. It's fun just being around this person. Their personality is attractive to you. You identify with this person deeply. You want to get to know them better. **There are no strings attached. You want nothing specific from him or her but a great friendship.** You want to spend more time with this person. You enjoy their company. **You say to yourself, "I find this person likable." You see Christ in him or her.** This is a person you would want as a best friend. Let's look at **Proverbs 17:17 KJV:** *A friend loveth at all times, and a brother is born for adversity.* **This feeling must also be mutual for a relationship to work.**

Second, is **"LUST"**, we can refer to this as a deep passion or deep **desire** as well. This means a strong yearning for another; it is a genuine longing for this other person. **Biblically, the Greek word here would be *(Erotas or Eros), meaning erotic love, sexual passion,* and intimate love.** Desiring him or her so much as to want to sexually devour this person; this may seem primitive, but true. You long for and desire everything about this person. This is a genuine physical attraction. You would lick him or her from head to toe, so to speak. You are attracted to something about him or her that takes your breath away. You desire him or her second only to the desire you have for God. Let's look at **Song of Solomon 7:10 NKJV** *I am my beloved's, And his desire is toward me.* This must be an exclusive desire for the one you want to marry. **This feeling must also be mutual for a relationship to work.**

Lastly, there's **"LOVE"**; this word in today's world has been so deluded and watered down to mean little. It was meant by God to be the greatest of all gifts. The greatest of all attributes. This trait is the highest and deepest of all personal feelings. This "love" is as deep for him or her as charity is, without needing anything in return. **Biblically, the Greek word here would be *(Agape)*, which means unconditional love.** This is the Love of God to send Jesus, His Only Son, to die. Loving someone is to die for them, if need be. **This is placing him or her first in your life, after God.** This is placing him or her before even oneself. This love is rare; it is needed in a relationship to make it work. **Many confuse love with lust.** When there is merely lust, that relationship is headed for disaster. **The love towards him or her must be unquenchable and sincere.** It must be able to withstand the storms of life, the *"ebb and flow."* **Let's refer to 1 Corinthians 13:4-7 KJV** *(4) Charity suffereth long, and is kind; charity envieth not; charity vaunteth not itself, is not puffed up,* The closest true Greek and Hebrew version of the Bible is the King James Version. Let me prove it here; other versions lack clarity and a precise definition of the accurate translation of Greek and Hebrew. Notice in the above verse that the word **CHARITY** is not the same as "love," which all the other versions of the Bible use. Love is an overused word; it's a two-way street for most. You love me, so I love you too, kind of thing. I love my cat, dog, or my ice cream sandwich. But **Charity is very different; it's a one-way street!** Have you ever given something to someone and expected nothing back in return? Have you ever given money to a homeless man? Did you get a receipt? Have you ever helped someone you knew could never repay you? That's Charity, and that type of commitment to each other is what's needed. *(5) Doth not behave itself unseemly, seeketh not her own, is not easily provoked, thinketh no evil;* Here we see that such love (charity) is not easily provoked; it's all in for one's spouse. *(6) Rejoiceth not in iniquity, but rejoiceth in the truth;* Charity (true love) only wants the truth, hates what God hates, and loves what God loves. *(7) Beareth all things, believeth all things, hopeth all things, endureth all things.* This type of love (charity) can endure all of life's ups and downs and will not be thwarted.

This feeling must also be mutual for a relationship to work.

If a person were to have only two of the three "L's," this is not a sufficient foundation on which to build a successful marriage.

All THREE "L's" MUST BE VISIBLE IN BOTH THE WOMAN AND IN THE MAN BEFORE MARRIAGE.

Chapter 4

Identify a Born-Again Believer

(Three Groups of People)

This is undoubtedly the single most important factor in choosing whom to date, leading to courting and marriage. Again, REAL Christians NEVER date to just date; we date looking for a spouse, period. I will explain the huge difference between being genuinely Born Again by God and simply thinking you are. *Imagine three groups of people.*

The First group of people consists of those who don't obviously care about Jesus as their Lord and Savior. They say Jesus is not God. **This group also comprises all false belief systems worldwide.** This group is very, very massive; the gate is very, very wide, leading to destruction *(Hell)*. This gate is wide for many reasons. Most religions are work-based. **This group may be very, very religious or even atheist.** Satan has and is using religions to push everyone away from the Biblical God. Those who use God's Law (Old Testament) must use it as a mirror, which will only damn them. Some in this group are still waiting for the *Messiah*. Judaism is a religion of Satan. The Law reveals their sin and condemns them as well. Many in this group think they are good enough to go to Heaven; they are not. No one is. They weigh their good and their bad, hoping to be good enough. God says in **Isaiah 64:6 NIV** *All of us have become like one who is unclean, and all our righteous acts are like filthy rags; we all shrivel up like a leaf, and like the wind our sins sweep us away.* **We see that on our best day, we are a Filthy**

Rag in front of a Holy and Righteous God. This group has no hope because they do not want the God of the Bible. This group is without God, without Jesus. God only allows perfection into Heaven. There is no one perfect but Jesus. **This group does not want Jesus to control their lives.** This group is NOT concerned with spiritual or eternal matters.

This group loves the world or the world system. This group loves themselves or their false idols. Many in this group are their own gods. This group worships false gods, a false jesus, and believes in false doctrines. This group has idols of their heart. Their idols are things they love more than God and fear more than God. They love and serve their idols more than God. **This group uses God's name as a curse word. They hate Christ because they love their sin.** These groups of people from this first group would all deny that Jesus is the only way to Father God. They are all identified as going against this verse of Scripture, John 14:6 NASB: Jesus *said, "I am the way, and the truth, and the life; no one comes to the Father except through Me.* **Those in this group are hell-bound and are a mixed bag of the above.**

The Second group of people consists of cosmetic "Christians." This group consists of those who honestly believe they're saved. **They chose God.** They may have said a prayer, walked an aisle, or had someone tell them they were born again *(note small b & a).* A fool may have told them, *"Welcome to the Family."* **This group says they belong to God's Family, but upon closer scrutiny, there is little family resemblance.** There are many who believe they're saved based on a verse or two from God's Word they cling to. A "pastor" claimed they were saved. They may be Catholics who buy into the creation of statues and images, referring to Exodus 20:4 GNT: *"Do not make for yourselves images of anything in heaven or on earth or in the water under the earth."* Here we read the second Commandment of God. **It is clear NOT to create ANY** *(pictures or statues)* **images of anything in Heaven; Jesus is in Heaven!** There are many that have some man figure on a cross; Jesus is off the cross! Catholics love to have statues and pictures. They also display a "Jesus" with **long hair; this is yet another disgrace to the Living God!** This is **1 Corinthians 11:14 ESV**: Does not nature itself teach you that if a man wears long hair, it is a **disgrace for him**? It is again plain to see that any man with long hair is disgraceful. **Jesus did NOT have long hair.** He was never a disgrace to His Father; any man with long hair is showing a dishonor to God. **In my other book, "It's All Subject to God's Word,"** includes a chapter on Why Catholics are NOT Christians, 10 intriguing chapters, such as Babies die and then what? Chapters on Cessationism, how to choose the *right* Church, Biblical Jargon exposed, and much, much more! Get that book as well!

Christians are to set the example of how to worship God in Spirit and in TRUTH. When a person worships in any way other than in Biblical Truth, pertaining to the God of the Bible, they are having a false "god", false doctrine, and a false "jesus". This group denies the **Five Solas** *(explained on page 166)*. This group adds works to salvation.

Some in this second group attend the correct Bible-teaching churches. **Remember, Judas hung out with Jesus *(God)* for three years and ended up belonging to Satan.** Again, many in this group come from Pentecostal or Charismatic backgrounds, most of whom agree with Biblical Truths, including the Trinity. They come from numerous "Christian" or non-denominational "churches." They even believe Jesus is who He said He was, God! Their worship is theatrical, superficial, and shallow, lacking Biblical Truth. They may be Biblically intellectual and even able to quote Scripture. These people could be "pastors" and may teach the Bible in their neighborhood church. They know God's Word and have studied it; they go to "church," some went to "seminary." They may have Bible verses written on their cars or on the walls at home. They know the Gospel yet have a different "jesus", a different faith, a different and false understanding of God's Truth.

They profess "Jesus" as their Lord. They listen to televangelists and receive their teachings from those shameless frauds. Those who listen to religious broadcasting networks like *TBN, Daystar,* and *Word of Faith* or *New Age-type* movements are really listening to Satan. He is the prince of those airwaves. Let's turn to **Ephesians 2:2 NKJV** *in which you once walked according to the course of this world, according to the prince of* *the power of the air, the spirit who now works in the sons of disobedience...* Here, Paul is explaining how we *(the Saved)* once were *(lost)* and who we listened to before God awakened us, before being Born Again. We walked in the ways of Satan, who controls the airwaves as in "fake news" as in "false information" as in "false doctrines" as in "false preachers". **These airwaves are always being used greatly by Satan. This group listens and follows the prince of the power of the air, Satan.**

Satan's armies of false teachers are selling countless lies, propagating Biblical errors daily. **They tell crowds of unlearned Biblically ignorant people that God will heal them. God will give them Heaven, wealth, and countless material things in return for their hard-earned money.** This group wants a Savior from Hell and a Santa Claus, but not a Savior from their sin. **This group loves to be entertained**; solid Biblical Doctrine is not their cup of tea. **Those in this second group are the hardest to reach and to witness to.** They are the ones who tell you they already know Jesus. They say, "Don't judge me". Let's again visit **2 Timothy 3:16 KJV** *All scripture is given by inspiration of God, and is profitable for doctrine, for reproof, for **correction**, for instruction in righteousness:* **We are instructed by GOD to judge and to correct others using scripture. There's Biblical ignorance, and then there's Biblical arrogance; this group has both.** This group defends God's Word only when convenient. When they do defend it, it's in a watered-down, twisted way. **This group consists of those who belong to or are associated with corrupted and adulterated churches.**

Those in this group say they, too, are born again but hate to be questioned on it or about it. **Truth does not mind being questioned, but a lie does not like being challenged.** They buy into "free will" towards Salvation. They profess they chose Jesus, or accepted Jesus, or made a decision for Jesus. **They asked Jesus into their heart. They say they are good people who let Jesus in.** They say Jesus was knocking, and they answered. They say Jesus is such a gentleman and would never make anyone believe. I will again quote Charles Spurgeon, *"We believe that the work of Regeneration, Conversion, Sanctification and Faith, is not an act of man's free will and power but of the mighty, efficacious and irresistible GRACE of God."* Brother Charles was spot on! **Simply ask** *(your date),* **"Whose choice was your Salvation?"** This group will answer by taking some credit for the reasonableness of an effort or decision **they made** directly and personally. This group would therefore answer the above question using a personal pronoun.

This group may have even been baptized. **I was baptized at nineteen years old and insisted I was saved then, but I was lost and deceived.** This group believes "Jesus" is a good addition to their lives. They may have stopped drinking or doing drugs. They also may be ex-criminals who credit "god" for their "new, better life." They have cleaned up their lives *(cleaned up their act)* and credit their change to "Jesus," and some are positive thinkers. They may have even stopped getting tattoos. Some men have stopped getting body piercings and have cut their long hair. This group lowers God's standards only to raise their own; some believe they are little "gods." **There are many in this group that are moved and motivated by demons, not God. This group tells people God loves** everyone. **This group sells love, love, love, but doesn't expose sin, sin, sin.** They may have heard of a miracle or say they seen some; and/or believe in someone's story. They read books from false teachers and cling to false, unbiblical beliefs.

There are many who believe some people went to Hell or Heaven and came back to write a book! These false prophets flatter people in their sins because they love to be flattered. This group consists mostly of liberal democrats and socialists. **This group loves to marginalize God's Word.** When you ask them how they were saved, they will mention something they did, said, allowed, chose, or accepted. That, again, would be salvation through works, which is another "Jesus." Salvation is by a God-given Faith alone; this Faith is also from God. If one adds any human effort, including prayer, to Salvation, it is no longer a free gift. **This group would disagree with the Doctrines of Grace** *(explained on page 162).* The book I wrote, "Digging Deeper into God's Truth Defines a Christian," covers that doctrine and more. Get a copy! Some in this group are hypocritical regarding God's moral issues. **This group seems to look and act like real Christians, and acknowledges who God is, while refusing to walk in His ways; so, does Satan.**

They say Amen a lot, some say Hallelujah a lot. They buy into the apostles' gifts today; they even say they, too, have apostolic gifts of their own. They call themselves modern-day prophets and apostles. They say they can cast out demons. They also say they can raise the dead. There are others that can heal you or even curse you in Jesus' name! **My book, titled "It's All Subject To God's Word," has several chapters on such**

topics; get that book as well. This group has a different "Jesus", a false "Jesus". They even think it is okay to listen to women "preachers." They say they can speak "tongues." I have personally tried to help this group and teach them Biblical Truths, hoping to reach out and correct members in this lost group countless times. Biblical Truths mean nothing if the person listening does not understand them, and only God opens their ears to hear. I realized after a long while that they were spiritually dead. **Biblical Truths do not raise the dead, Biblical Wisdom or logic does not raise the dead! Repeating God's Truths over and over or arguing with them or even using common sense, does NOT raise the Spiritually DEAD.** I spent many, many hours with many explaining correct Doctrine using Bible chapters and verses, to no avail. **These groups of lost people would rather turn a teachable moment into an argument, rather than be Biblically Corrected.** Many are puffed up with pride. **They are abandoned by God, left by God to their own demise.** Let's look at **2 Timothy 4:3 ESV** *For the time is coming (it's here) when people will not endure sound teaching but having itching ears they will accumulate for themselves teachers to suit their own passions.*

There was one Pentecostal woman; this one time, from this group where God openly used my efforts. My efforts were acknowledged and were fruitful because of God. I am thankful on this side of Heaven that God allowed me to see His transforming results of some of my futile efforts. I witnessed the consequences of my seeds of His truths, where my words of boldness (which are His) were able to bring me to witness and plainly perceive God's Fruits of change. I was on a date; she and I went for a long walk on the beach in Fort Lauderdale, Florida.

This was years before I met my current wife. She told me she was a "pastor." She went on to say she spoke in "tongues." The sole reason I went on that date was that I did not understand how to vet. I went after looks first, not God first! That night, God wanted me to date this lady for His reasons. When a person sees why God allows something that benefits Him, it's truly exciting! Frankly, most of the time we never see our efforts or seeds come to fruition. These conversions and transformations are all from Him. It's just from time-to-time that God allows us to be used in the planting of "Truth Seeds." It's ALL Him working in and through us. God's Fruit of His Truths can and will be used by Him through us to open the eyes of ONLY His Elect. We walked on that beach, and we talked for hours. **I used scripture to explain that she was not a "pastor" and her "tongues" were false. She wasn't too happy with my candor.** I was using God's Word to challenge her false understanding of scripture. This particular story is detailed in my book, *"Digging Deeper into God's Truth Defines a Christian."*

I will now get to the point at hand. We parted that one night; I had her phone number, and she had mine. **I moved on searching for Miss Right; day by day, one date at a time.** Six months had passed when I received a phone call from this young lady. She asked if I remembered her. I said to her, " Of course, I do and asked how she was doing." She openly confessed, "Doing much better after what you told me six months earlier." **She said, "God used you to open my eyes to Him". She went on saying, "I am not a pastor, nor could any woman be." She added, "I cannot speak in tongues nor could I ever."** I was in a moment of awe, a moment of silence. I knew God was on that phone in both our hearts. **I knew then why God planted me on**

that date six months earlier. During that revealing phone call from her, **I witnessed an old life shifting from Satan's lies into God's Truth.**

God was openly revealing His Miraculous Power and His Love to us both. God does His Work in the hearts of His Children, His Elect. It was a God moment. This lady was speaking from her *new heart,* explaining the talk we had months earlier, which God used to awaken her from her spiritually dead, darkened self to His Light. **She was truly converted from her lost state of mind, which I had found her in six months earlier. God's Truth set her free, free from false doctrines.** She was excited to finally be in God's Truth; such is God's impact. She told me she just had to call me to tell me I was right. I told her thank you, and I prayed with her on the phone. I professed it was all God, and she agreed. I said good-bye to her, and we never spoke again. **I was in her life for that one reason, that one moment, that realization by God, for God.** She was brought into His Light and His Truth by Him. **It was a moment of confirmation for me, a moment that explains why we, as Christians, do what we do. Speak up all the time for God's Truths, in season or out of season.**

We know we will offend many, insult many, and we will lose friends, family, and those who have their own god. Then quickly realizing we are NOT here for the many, NOT here for the world. **We are NOT here to condone the lies**, NOT here to go along with Biblical falsehoods. **We are NOT here to babysit the lost, but we are here to be bold in the Truth for Him and to feed His Sheep.** Often, the best thing you can do for someone who is lost is to tell them God's Truth. Then back away, pray deeply for them, and let God do what ONLY He can do in their lives. When this lady thanked me for my words of Truth that day, I said to her it was all God, and it was…

This reminds me of **Matthew 16:13-17 LB** *(13) When Jesus came to Caesarea Philippi, he asked his disciples, "Who are the people saying I am?" (14) "Well," they replied, "some say John the Baptist; some, Elijah; some, Jeremiah or one of the other prophets." (15) Then he asked them, "Who do you think I am?" (16) Simon Peter answered, "The Christ, the Messiah, the Son of the living God." (17) "God has blessed you, Simon, son of Jonah," Jesus said, "for my Father in heaven has personally revealed this to you—this is not from any human source.* **Remembering to plant seeds of Biblical Truth is a Christian's natural responsibility, but to open someone's eyes to God's Truth is Supernatural.** We should also know that without receiving the Holy Spirit, no one's eyes are truly open; only partially open. The Holy Spirit was only available to God's Elect after His Resurrection and His ascent back to Heaven. This refers to **John 14:16-17 NASB** *(16) I will ask the Father, and He will give you another Helper, so that He may be with you forever; (17) the Helper is the Spirit of Truth, whom the world cannot receive, because it does not see Him or know Him; but you know Him because He remains with you and will be in you.*

This second group does NOT have the Holy Spirit. This group has many who will know and defend half of the Bible. **Their fruit is ungodly; they create more false converts, more false teachers, more woman preachers, and more false doctrines.** They regularly listen to false teaching; some have for generations. They believe what others told them *(i.e., pastors, teachers, and family)*. **They love the hype and excitement of false movements and entertainment churches.** They love the "Prosperity Gospel" and believe in the "Name it and Claim it doctrine." This group does not understand the Holy Spirit. They think His job is to make them act like fools, but His job is to create in True Believers a Christ-like character. **The "churches" of today have become playgrounds and theatres, even social hangouts, NOT places of sound Theology. They feed a gospel to their congregations from a rebellious freewill table of nonsense Jesus would flip over!**

Many in this group buy into the three major sins: the lust of the eyes, the lust of the flesh, and the boastful pride of life. They seek God's Hand, not His Face. They belong to the "fivefold ministry." They misinterpret and distort God's Word habitually. They teach others lies, knowingly or unknowingly. **They seek what God can do for them, yet don't seek God.** They display pictures, images, or statues of their god. Some people love the loud "music," including a light show, and call it their "church." **They attend a "church" as spectators would visit a Broadway show.** We cannot entertain anyone into the Kingdom. This group buys into "tithing," giving their money to charlatans. **This group plays spiritual gymnastics with Scripture, twisting it constantly.** They think God is their "genie in a bottle." **This group uses countless false narratives to draw false converts to a false christ (note the small "c").**

This second group rejects God's doctrine of Election; they are even offended by it! They are the lost and confused; such confusion comes from Satan. They buy into *"Arminian"* theology, which is straight poison. They would argue God's Sovereignty. *This group practices Eisegesis.* They twist Biblical Truths to suit their cult or false religious beliefs. There is No Bible twister that will inherit the Kingdom of God. The Kingdom of Heaven is not for clever liars. This group goes through the motions of being a Christian, but they are counterfeit Christians. A believer who lacks understanding of God's Sovereignty and human depravity cannot express the true significance of the Gospel. **Those in this group are also hell-bound and are a mixed bag of the above.**

A few from this group do become Saved. Yes, therefore, there is a remnant. **Ignorance of Scripture is the root of every error and heresy.** If one is truly saved by God, he or she absolutely understands this chapter regarding these three groups. If true conversion is not evident, those reading this are still in this second or first group. **There is no way to know you are in the third group, unless you understand how completely lost and helpless the entire first and second group are, and how lost you were while in them.** I was in this second group for over twenty-five years! This group is identified in Scripture, let's again refer to **Matthew 7:21-23 NKJV** *(21) "Not everyone who says to Me, 'Lord, Lord,' shall enter the kingdom of heaven, but he who does the will of My Father in heaven. (22) Many will say to Me in that day, 'Lord, Lord, have we not prophesied in Your name, cast out demons in Your name, and done many wonders in Your name?' (23) And then I will declare to them, 'I never knew you; depart from Me, you who practice lawlessness!'* **Those in this group are also referred to as the *Tares* among the *Wheat.***

59

I want to point out the Biblical understanding of what God means by the *Wheat* and the *Tares.* Let's see **Matthew 13:30 NKJV** *Let both grow together until the harvest, and at the time of harvest I will say to the reapers, "First gather together the tares and bind them in bundles to burn them, but gather the wheat into my barn."* **Here, Jesus is explaining the Parable of the Wheat and Tares. The "Wheat" are those belonging to Him, His Children, His Elect. The "Tares" are those planted *(in Christian churches or among true Believers)* who belong to Satan.** Satan mingles his children with God's, and in some cases, it's almost impossible to distinguish between the two. Satan knows the Bible very well. They appear to be true Believers, but they are not. Jesus says, Don't worry, when the time comes, the **TARES** will be thrown into Hell for eternity. The **WHEAT** will go with Him *(Jesus)* to Heaven for eternity.

It stands to reason and Biblical scrutiny that God has enough power to convert a cold, lost heart and enough power to redeem a lost, wicked, and useless sinner. God has enough power to save a person's soul from His Own Wrath; each, of course, is a miracle. **Therefore, God has enough power to also bring the ones who are truly His into His Truth and bring them out from all the cults, false doctrines, and all false teachers and teachings.** *God did this concerning the woman I walked with on the beach.* If God chooses not to change a person's heart, it's because He gives them over to their own morally corrupt mind. Go now to **Romans 1:28 NIV** *Furthermore, just as they did not think it worthwhile to retain the knowledge of God, so God gave them over to a depraved mind, so that they do what ought not to be done.* **This is obvious and is the most fearsome act of God's Judgment on this side**

of life. He simply gives people over to their own *(depraved, wicked, corrupt, and morally degenerate)* minds. I believe God does this to further expose those we, as Believers, should separate from. Let's look at **Matthew 7:6 NASB:** *"Do not give what is holy to dogs, and do not throw your pearls before pigs, or they will trample them under their feet, and turn and tear you to pieces.* **Here we are taught to Judge Biblically.** Don't continue to give the Truth to those who hate the truth. If you continue to witness to those who hate you, they will want to take your life.

Those of unbelief; those of the world who were NOT of God's Elect have murdered every Prophet and Apostle but John. **The world killed Jesus *(who is God Incarnate)* on the cross. You should expect no better if you are a True Believer.** If you are **not** a real Christian, this does not apply to you. During the reading of this book, if you discover you are not saved; beg Jesus to bury the old you so He can rise up in your life. Cry out to Him over and over again. Read and study the Gospel of John, over and over. If God speaks to your heart, you will know. If you long to be a True Believer, please email me personally, **and I will pray for your salvation as well. Seriously.**

The Devil is not fighting false religions *(he created them all)* or unbelief *(on our own, that's all we have),* as clarified in the first group. He is much too smart for that. Satan has been and is producing a counterfeit "Christianity" which is identified in the second group. **Satan's false "Christianity" is so much like the real thing that most True Christians are afraid to speak out against it.** I am not, nor should YOU be. This group wants a Jesus of their own making. **I was in this**

second group, and I did not think I was lost either. Satan is a genius. I was removed from this group by God. I am now in Christ, for Christ. **I am bought with the Highest Price ever, the** *(blood of Christ);* **I am not my own.** The people we keep giving God's Truths to, hoping and praying God will open their eyes to Him. Sadly, it often only hardens them further.

The Third group of people consists of those whom God Has Chosen, His Chosen, His Elected Individuals, His Children. These are the traits you want and are looking for in and from your next date or current relationship. These are the only True Born Again Believers. They were all chosen by God according to the Good Pleasure of His *(God's)* Will. They all would profess that each had nothing to do with their own Salvation. They fully comprehend that Salvation is ALWAYS 100% GOD and ZERO % man. **They have a teachable Spirit. They are a sponge for God's Truths.** They also wear a bulletproof vest concerning false teaching. They would all profess they are wretched sinners and how unworthy each truly is to be saved. **They recognize their sins and understand that true repentance is followed by obedience.** This group recognizes that repentance is not simply the start of the Christian life; it is the Christian life. This group knows there is no Synergism *(involving a person's collaboration)* concerning their Salvation. They believe in Monergism *(a theological doctrine that regeneration is exclusively the work of the Holy Spirit).* They recognize sin and acknowledge God's Wrath. They understand the process of Justification. **They seek God's Wisdom from His Holy Word daily. This group defends God's Word 24/7.** They all know that they are responsible for fully obeying God's Word and boldly proclaiming His Truths. **They stand in opposition to the current culture.** They have an unyielding desire to spread the Gospel. This group does not hide from tough Biblical questions.

Let's check out **1 Peter 3:15 NKJV** *But sanctify the Lord God in your hearts, and always be ready to give a defense to everyone who asks you a reason for the hope that is in you, with meekness and fear...* This group knows their Bible. If there is a question he or she does not know, they will start a study on it. They are ready to answer truthfully what God's Word says and truly means. This is the love of Truth concerning this group. This group understands that if they are not in a war with their sin, they are not saved. They recognize they are redeemed and transformed by the power of God, not themselves. They have a renewed mind that hates sin and loves God's Word. They love living in their transformation. **They love to learn about Christ and love His Laws. They have a new self. The old self in them is dead.**

What comes to mind here is one of my favorite quotes from John Calvin *(Theologian, Pastor, and Reformer).* ***"A dog barks when his master is attacked. I would be a coward if I saw that God's Truth is attacked and yet would remain silent."*** This group does NOT remain silent when they hear or witness lifestyles, concepts, statements, or half-truths that go against God's Word. **There are times this group becomes as Christ-like as to literally turn over tables,** while supporting, enforcing, and standing up for God's Truths. **This group is not afraid to lose family or friends over God. God is their first priority.** Their joy is to dig deep into their Bibles, moving closer to God each day in Spirit and in **Truth**. They would defend God's entire Word, all sixty-six books. They realize defending God's Word is not like playing with a *toy boat in a bathtub*. It's more like being engaged in a *war with a battleship*.

The True Church is not an audience to be entertained, but an ARMY to be empowered. Those in this group are called seemingly harsh names by the world, such as *"Radical," "Jesus Freak," "Super Christian," "Calvinist," "Fanatical," "Extremist," "Bible Thumper," "Crazy,"* or *"Dogmatic."* These are simply some of the **names false believers use** to describe this group. **These are, in reality, minimum requirements which identify True Christians, who are spiritually AWAKE in a lost, insane, and fallen world.** If Jesus walked the earth today, such labels would be placed on Him as well. **People who call others such names are themselves phony;** they are lovers of this world rather than lovers of God. **There are real fanatics; those are the ones in the *second group* that won't listen or adhere to Biblical Truths. They take their twisted, false doctrines to extremes, imposing their deceptions on others.**

Let's look at **Matthew 11:11 ESV** *Truly, I say to you, among those born of women there has arisen no one greater than John the Baptist.* Here, Jesus is explaining what He thought of John the Baptist. Many people of that time and today would say John was a true FANATIC. Jesus says he was the best of the best, born of a woman. **Some people may say you are strongly opinionated when you simply quote scripture.** This is evident because most "christians" today are not Born Again by God and therefore are NOT true Christians at all. Remember, John the Baptist lost his head for having a Biblical view of marriage.

Those in this Third group know Jesus is much more than an *addition* to their lives; *He is their Life!* The God of the Bible is their God (Jesus), and they are His Children. This group loves God and recognizes God's sovereignty. They love to witness to the lost. **They have a burden for lost souls.** This group knows The Father, The Son, and The Holy Spirit. They have a thirst and a longing for God in their soul. **They use Christ as their compass. They don't have to "get in touch" with God; they live in touch with God.** They know they are sinners and sin against a Holy and Righteous God. They know they too deserve Hell, yet recognize the Mercy and Grace of God. **They did not ask Jesus into their hearts; Jesus changed their hearts radically, without their permission.** They are transformed by God to believe and understand scripture. **They believe and comprehend with joy all the Doctrines of Grace.** They hate the world in its fallen state. They hate what God hates and love what God loves, and they know the difference. **They are hated by the world**.

Let's read **Matthew 10:22 ESV,** *and you will be hated by all for my name's sake. But the one who endures to the end will be saved.* Jesus says here you will be **hated** by ALL. This means all who are NOT His. **If you are NOT hated at least by some, examine yourself to see if you are in the CORRECT Faith.** This group is God's Chosen people. They despise and expose *"Marshmallow Christians and weak Pastors"* who never preach on or mention Election, Sin, Hell, or God's Wrath.

Those in this group pass Biblical Truths on to others; such is their fruit. **They are able and willing to judge others and all things by God's standards, not the world's.** They are understandably NOT popular with the first or second group. **This group exposes false truths, false pastors, false idols, false doctrines, and false teachers, which the first and second groups love, follow, listen to, look up to, and adore.**

I have been associated with several denominations throughout my years of learning. The *Christian Reformed Church* is today's most Biblical Church. **Reformed Theology claims the whole Bible is God's Word and teaches the whole Bible.** They firmly believe the Truths of the *Doctrines of Grace.* They believe in the full Counsel of God. They believe God is a Saving God who is Holy, Righteous, and Sovereign. They believe God's Word is final and absolute. They believe in Sovereign Election, which is Bible 101 and is evident throughout Scripture. Charles Spurgeon once said, *"Reformed Theology is just a nickname for Biblical Christianity".* **We must be grounded and rooted in the *good soil* of Scripture; Reformed Theology does that.**

This group practices Exegesis *(the legitimate interpretation of a text).* This group lives to glorify God. This group exalts Christ. They do not tolerate false Doctrine. **They never stand up for sin, but always call sin out and oppose it.** They love God's Sovereignty and understand human depravity. **They teach others to observe all things Jesus has commanded. They bear good fruit, and they feed Biblical Truths to other Disciples, who consequently teach the same Biblical Truths.** They love others and are humble. Sound

Doctrine produces loving people. Humility is submitting to the Will of God. **They realize that truth with love is at times punishing, but love without Truth is hypocrisy. We know love and Truth are both necessary.** The opposite of Truth is not simply error, but sin. **There is no such thing as "Truth-less" love.** This group laments over their own moral and Spiritual failures. **This group doesn't merely know what God expects and wants, but knows God.** Those in this group are God's Sheep. They are drawn closer to God *(not by motivational speakers)* by the hard, hard Truths of God's Word. This may sound harsh or unbearable to those with their own contemporary worldly receptiveness.

This group is unwavering in its commitment to Biblical Truths. **This group fully understands Salvation is Trinitarian, being Chosen by God the Father, Redeemed by Jesus the Son, and Called by the *Holy Spirit.*** This group showcases God's Love in Truth and listens to **Expository Preachers** who use scripture to cover the entire text or passage. **This group loves and accepts real Biblical Correction, even thanks those who correct them; they understand that it's better to be divided by Truth than united in error.** They know they have a responsibility to grow more spiritually in God's Truth each day. They understand God's love and fear God. This group is among the 3% of Christians who have read all 66 books of the Bible and continue to read and study the Bible daily.

Those in this group are themselves deeply knowledgeable theologians who will rightly defend Scripture. They love God's Children *(His Elect)*. **This group is**

much, much smaller than one could ever imagine. This group is identified in Scripture in **Ephesians 1:4-5 NASB** *(4) just as He (God) chose us in Him before the foundation of the world, that we (His Elect) would be holy and blameless before Him. In love (5) He predestined us (His Elect) to adoption as sons and daughters through Jesus Christ to Himself, according to the good pleasure of His Will (God's Will).* This group has all their Faith in Jesus the Christ, their Faith is *from God,* and they know they are going to Heaven. *This group is the Light and Salt of the earth.* **Those in this group are Heaven Bound and are the Wheat among the Tares.**

In a nutshell, if there is no drastic change, no conversion, one is still dead in their sins. **I was a make-believer for over 25 years before God Truly Saved me.** I was a make-believer; I looked and played the part of a Christian. **The difference is that when you are saved, you long for Biblical Correction. Your heart is transformed.** You love Jesus and His Word and hate sin, not just sin's consequences. You love God's Truths and seek them like Gold each day. **You will lose friends and family and be hated, not loved.** You will again have a newfound, sincere burden for lost souls. You learn the Bible; you understand and agree with the *Doctrines of Grace*. **You realize you had NOTHING to do with your first or second Birth.** *If you did something towards your own Salvation, it's fake.* Salvation is ALWAYS 100% God and 0% man. Let's turn to **Ephesians 2:8-9 NASB** *(8) For by grace you have been saved through faith; and this is **not** of yourselves, it is the gift of God; (9) not a result of works, so that no one may boast.* Here, the Apostle Paul is addressing Believers. He is explaining Salvation, stating both **God's Grace and Saving Faith are both directly from God.** This is a Gift from God. God's Grace and Faith can only be received with empty hands.

God has created Salvation in a way where no one Saved could possibly take ANY credit. There was or is nothing you can do to deserve His Grace, such is Grace. **Therefore, there is no such thing as free will towards Salvation. Those who buy into that lie are themselves still lost and without God's Grace.** Salvation is ALL God, or it's not from God. If someone adds to Salvation their "decision" or their "repentance" or their "baptism" or their "free-will" or any other type of "work" or any personal pronouns whatsoever, it's NOT the Gospel according to Scripture. **Jesus paid it ALL; even your sanctification is of Him. Either you believe that, or your faith is in vain.** Salvation is all God's will. Let's read **Ephesians 1:5 NASB** *He (GOD) predestined us (HIS ELECT) to adoption as sons and daughters through Jesus Christ to Himself, according to the good pleasure of His Will...***Please Read this Again HIS (GOD'S) WILL, not my will, not your will, and not free-will.** If someone claims to be a Christian yet never challenges false doctrine, you MUST question their faith. **True Christians cannot tolerate false doctrines. Free-will Salvation (Arminianism) is called easy-believism, which is a false doctrine (gospel) from Satan.**

False doctrines only create false Christians (false converts); only the Truth will set you free. The one who is Born Again by God, such are His Elect. Let's open up now to **1 Corinthians 4:7 NASB** *For who considers you as superior? What do you have that you did not receive? And if you did* *receive it, why do you boast as if you had not received it?* Here, we MUST understand God is Sovereign. There is nothing given to you that is not from God; neither you nor I is any more important than anyone else. There is no one who is above another to boast of what he or she has. All things good and bad are from God. This includes His Wrath, His Gospel, His Love, His Judgment, and **His Salvation.** Therefore, Salvation is ALL from God, period. Everything today is all about Jesus, but we must know Him in Truth. Quoting Charles Spurgeon, *"Giving your heart to Christ is not the Gospel. Salvation comes from something that Christ gives you, not something that you give to Christ."* **We can't take ANY credit in any capacity for a person's Salvation; that only proves they're still lost.** When someone is truly saved, they become a better person, absolutely. However, Jesus did not die to make me or you a better person. **He died to save my Soul from His Wrath in Hell and for me to live my life to glorify Him, not myself.** Quoting John MacArthur (Pastor/Author/Theologian), *"If you trust in your own goodness, you are doomed. God accepts only absolute perfection, which does not exist in the human realm, except in Christ." Remember This***: God Saved His Elect from Himself for Himself and all by Himself.**

Chapter 5

Don't Lean on John 3:16

Those of you here who may disagree with Election; disagree with the Bible. Some here even believe that Jesus died for all people. There are some, like I once was, who believe that a simple prayer or a personal belief is enough in Jesus to be saved from God's Wrath. True Christians want to be saved for God's Use and live righteously for His Glory. Let's look at **Mark 4:11-12 NKJV** *(11) And He said to them, "To you (the Elect) it has been given to know the mystery of the kingdom of God; but to those who are outside (the lost), all things come in parables, (12) so that Seeing they may see and not perceive, And hearing they may hear and not understand; Lest they should turn, And their sins be forgiven them."* Here, Jesus explains why some understand Him and others do not. Those that are His *(Elect)* are given an understanding of scripture and an understanding of God's Truths, including His Election process.

Those who hear His Word, but never seem to fully accept or understand it all, but argue it, are still lost in their sins. There is no one who becomes saved through man's traditions, arguments, or Christian apologetics, or customs, or by Biblical half-truths, but by the whole Gospel. Let's visit **2 Corinthians 5:21 NKJV** *For He made Him who knew no sin to be sin for us, that we might become the righteousness of God in Him.* This verse speaks of Salvation only found in Jesus, who was born by the virgin birth and lived a sinless life. He dies at Calvary on a cross and three days later rose from the dead and lives; Jesus is God. We ALL sin every day, and such sins must not go unpunished by a Righteous and Holy God. I have heard people tell me they don't even sin! Let's skip to **1 John 1:8 KJV:** *If we say that we have no sin, we deceive ourselves, and the truth is not in us.* The Apostle John is making it crystal clear that we are ALL sinners. **Those who turn from their sins and live their whole remaining life for Jesus are His. What does that look like, you ask?**

1) The Bible says that to know you are Born Again by God (Saved) is to have a deep burden for other people's souls. *Do you?*

2) **The fruit of a True Believer is a newfound desire *(burden)* to give your family and all friends and even strangers the Gospel, praying to God for their Salvation daily!** *Do you?*

3) The fruit of Salvation is to always take a stand and rebuke and correct others who are for what God is against, which are abortion, gay rights, gay marriage, false teachers, and false doctrines. Christians are offended by what offends God. *Are you standing up verbally, speaking up, defending God's Word, or are you defending the world with your silence?*

4) We should have a better understanding of what it means to be a Christian; this means to love what God loves and hate what God hates. *Do you?*

5) The result of a converted heart by God is to accept and understand God did it all; Salvation is <u>NOT</u> by any works you did, or could do, or yet must do; or something you said. *Do you agree?*

6) Salvation is given only by God's Grace through Jesus. ***Do you agree?***

7) **The result of a Saved person is that they will always go out of their way to spread the biblical Gospel.** ***Do you?***

8) They will go out of their way to let all others know they are a Christian; this way, it is known and not hidden. There are no lukewarm Christians; those are the ones Jesus throws into Hell. ***Do you understand this?***

9) **We should plant seeds of God's Truth by giving out Bible Tracts** *(without the sinners' prayer!).* **Tell others of Jesus and express to others their <u>need</u> for Jesus; to all those they encounter. They are not ashamed to do this.** ***Are you doing this?***

10) They long to be used by God in countless ways. When their "friends" see them, they will say, "There go those Christians." ***Does this describe you?***

11) **When you do the *minimum requirements,* as in letting others around you know God's Truths, the world will soon hate you as they did Jesus.** The reason you teach and tell others of God's Truth, risking worldly friendships, is not because you're unkind or want attention or accolades, but for God's Glory. ***Are you hated by the world yet? If not, maybe you don't belong to Jesus? Examine yourself.***

12) When acting out Salvation, this starts with accepting Biblical Corrections joyfully. Christians are always growing in

God's Word because they are in It daily. ***Do you accept Biblical Correction? Are you in His Word daily?***

13) If a person is in a good Marital Relationship, there is constant communication between the husband and wife. When a person is in a Good Relationship with God, there is constant communication (through prayer and Bible study) concerning each Believer and Father God through Jesus Christ. Christians are always in constant communication with their Father. ***Are you?***

14) Most worldly people basically live for their fun activities, family times, money, or prestige at their workplace. The LOST don't put Jesus first in all they do. **You are either moving closer to God each day or further away.** The True Believer moves closer to God each day through His Holy Word. Let's look at **Colossians 3:17 NASB:** *whatever you do in word or deed, do everything in the name of the Lord Jesus, giving thanks through Him to God the Father.* The Apostle Paul teaches us how to live in Christ; this verse is self-explanatory. ***Do you live this way?***

Let's visit **John 6:37 NKJV** *All that the Father gives Me will come to Me, and the one who comes to Me I will by no means cast out.* Jesus is again explaining Election; those His Father gives Him, meaning each and every one He died for will be Saved. **Salvation is not a group of words put together to request His Salvation.** Many people use John 3:16 without even understanding the verse. Let's look at **John 3:16 NKJV** *For God so (in this way) loved the world that He gave His only begotten Son, that whoever believes in Him should not perish but have everlasting life.* The Greek word for "believes" is "pistis," meaning belief grounded in confidence and trust in God-given faith, and to continue believing (to no end). This Salvational Faith is ONLY from God and by God; not from, or by YOU. That would be a *false faith (self-induced)* leading to Hell, and not God's Effectual Faith. Therefore, no one should take a verse from here or there and build a doctrine on it. *This is why I write: to bring clarity to those who seek it.* I write to feed the Sheep. **There are too many who believe in a false "Christian life" based on cherry picking verses they like, but not living the Christian life in obedience, which God demands.** Let's really see who John 3:16 is referring to by looking at **John 17:9 KJV** *I pray for them: I pray not for the world, but for them which thou hast given me; for they are thine.* Here, we clearly see who Jesus is referring to in John 3:16, God's Elect, not the world, ONLY those His Father chose before the foundation of the world.

Jesus said you would know His Elect by their fruit; thus, this book. God so loved the world *(Greek word for World is Kosmos)* means the Nations, Tribes, kindreds of the world, not just the Jews, but also the Gentiles; this refers to the **world of BELIEVERS** *(God's Elect)* in contradistinction from "The world of the Ungodly." Let's look at **Psalm 73:12 KJV** *Behold, these are the ungodly, who prosper in the world; they increase in riches.* Let's look at **1 John 2:15 KJV** *Love not the world, neither the things that are in the world. If any man loves the world, the love of the Father is not in him.* This should clarify that John 3:16 is the most misunderstood verse among the unlearned or unconverted. Yet it brings peace to God's Elect because it is meant only for them. Many professing "Christians" live a life of doing what they want, when they want. They don't die to themselves but live for themselves. They blend into the world so well; most are loved by many because they are truly of the world. **They are "Christian" only in name.** Those are the false converts for whom I wrote this chapter. Maybe you are still alive today because God wants you to hear His FULL message. He wants to bring you down to your knees, crying out for His Mercy as I once did. God wants you to realize just Who He is and who you are not. True Believers are not boastful of their Salvation but thankful, because they know they did nothing for it; such is God's Grace. The fruit of Believers is evident if one knows how and what to look for.

What we should always do is test each Spirit to be certain it is of Christ; we are to be <u>fruit inspectors</u>. Undoubtedly, if I were to reduce *God's Election* to its simplest terms, it would mean that *God chose me before I chose Him.* There are also too many people who think, "That's it; I believe, so leave me alone!" I have heard others say, "Oh, stop with that Bible stuff," and "I have been up there; I am now on my way down, while you're still going up." There is never any going down, unless you mean Hell. When a person is saved by God, they are saved for God, and they want the privilege to be greatly and openly used by God. This is the evidence of Faith. Those who say, "I am Saved, go Save someone else," are people still dead in their sin, not Saved but lost and self-deceived. **I lived in that foolish mindset for over twenty-five years; that's how I can identify with it so well.** If that's you today, admit it, cry out to God through Jesus, and beg and keep begging for His Mercy and Grace concerning your sinful life. I suggest **reading the Gospel of John over and over and over.**

The type of Belief Jesus speaks of here in John 3:16 is a steadfast, ongoing Belief till death that doesn't waiver or weaken but strengthens until the day you die. Everyone is a Christian until the Guillotine comes out. Everyone is a Christian when it looks nice, but when it means going against family and friends, against all you once believed, well, that's a different story. Everyone is a Christian until it gets biblical. The people who have Jesus have nothing to lose in standing up for what's right, what's Biblical. This is how you know who His are, and who is of the world. **God's real Chosen People have always been called *fanatics*.** There was an old analogy I remember: If you were arrested for being a Christian, would there be enough evidence to convict you? What this simply means is, **"What are your fruits?"** If I went to your home right now, would there be Christian books, Bibles, and open writings concerning current Bible studies on your desk? The point here is that Believers never stop Believing, never stop growing, studying, learning, and expounding on what they already know. **Therefore, Christians are always in the Word; this is the life-long process of *Sanctification* concerning all True Believers, period.** Social media is also a good place to look, as it can offer a hint of what he or she truly believes in and what they focus on most.

Let's say you were not eating physical food for a month or two months; your body would die. Let's say you don't drink any water for 4 or 5 days; your body would die. This death is a physical death, which is real. The person who is not reading God's Word is not eating the *Bread of Life*, he or she is therefore Spiritually DEAD. The person who is not thirsty for Him and does not drink *His Living Water* daily is also Spiritually DEAD.

This is also REAL death. Let's look at **James 2:26 KJV** *For as the body without the spirit is dead, so faith without works is dead also.* When a person is Spiritually DEAD, only God's Mercy can save them. **Christians are never saved by good works but Saved to do good works.** Let's never get those two mixed up. A Christian's "good works" would include his or her fruits, which always come after Salvation by God, not before Salvation. Therefore, Christians do good works as a RESULT of our Salvation, not as a requirement for being Saved. The religions that claim or require one must do "this or that" to be saved are <u>ALL</u> cults and false religions created by Satan.

Let's look at **Romans 4:6** *ESV, just as David also speaks of the blessing of the one to whom God counts righteousness apart from works.* We see that King David was aware of God's Grace, so to better explain God's Grace concerning Election is to visualize the man hanging on the cross next to Jesus. This man did nothing in terms of any "good works." He was not baptized, he never went to Church, he was a thief, he was not good, he was a wicked sinner, and he gave no contribution as to merit Salvation whatsoever; neither do we. However, Jesus told him he would see him that day in Paradise; that's GOD'S ELECTION! Today, God's Word tells His Children the same thing. **How are we to know today that a person is Saved? We can only know by addressing the fruits of belief in actions, in word, and in God's <u>Truths</u>. The person who is not constantly praying to God and reading His Word has no Communication with Him.** When you read and study God's Word, He is talking to your heart. When you pray to Him, you are talking to Him in Spirit and in Truth. Both praying and reading His Word daily are both required; it's never one or the other. When Charles Spurgeon *was* asked, **"What is more important: praying or reading the Bible?"** Charles then asked, *"What is more important: breathing in or breathing out?"* **Ignorance of Scripture continues to be the root of every error in religion and the source of every heresy.** This is the reason I write. **If you want to follow Jesus, expect to be treated as Jesus was.** Satan has used countless religions to push everyone away from God's Truth. Quoting John MacArthur, *"I offend people all the time because that's necessary. If you try to develop a kind of Christianity that's inoffensive, that's not Christianity, it's not the Gospel."*

Charles Spurgeon, quoting George Whitefield, Preacher/Evangelist, 1700s, may have said it best, **"We are all born Arminians; it is Grace that turns us into Calvinists."** You see, without God's Mercy and His Grace, we would ALL go where we each belong: Hell. Let's recap what an *Arminian* truly is: he or she would be one who believes in free will towards salvation, which is a false doctrine. People have free will in essentially everything else, but not in Salvation. **If God's Salvation were left up to us, we would ALL be Hellbound!** I remember a statement from R.C. Sproul: someone once told him they were saved because of a decision they made. R.C. then replies, **"Let me get this straight, you're saved by grace, but it was up to you?" This expounds on the ridiculous** *Arminian* **mindset.**

Remember this: The Prophets and Apostles were not hated and put to DEATH for preaching "LOVE, LOVE, LOVE!" They were hated and KILLED for teaching GOD'S TRUTH!

Chapter 6

Marital Sex

This has been a subject most people shun. There are many people who have nothing or little to say about SEX; this includes most "Pastors and Christian writers" today. God has spoken on sex countless times; it's always been obvious and very frequent in the Bible, starting in Genesis. In **Genesis 1:27-28 ESV,** *So, God created man in his own image, in the image of God he created him; male and female he created them. And God blessed them. And God said to them, "Be fruitful and multiply and fill the earth and subdue it, and have dominion over the fish of the sea and over the birds of the heavens and over every living thing that moves on the earth."* Let's unpack these two verses; we see God created man in His Own image *(able to relate to God, able to interact with God as an ethical creature, one that could reason and have intellect)*. God created male and female, not changing or multiple genders, but **only** man and woman, period. **God wanted them to have plenty of sex, so they would multiply. Human beings are sexual creatures.** God gave them full authority and control over all the animals and creatures in the sea, the air, and on land.

Let's look at **Genesis 4:1-2 NASB** *Now the man had relations with his wife Eve, and she conceived and gave birth to Cain, and she said, "I have obtained a male child with the help of the Lord." And again, she gave birth to his brother Abel...*This verse demonstrates the first time there were results from sexual intercourse in the Bible, and each time God's Word says "went into" or "came into" or "knew" or "took a wife" or "make fruitful and multiply" or "go in unto her." This depends on what Bible version you are reading; such wordings refer to sex between a husband and a wife. In the Old Testament days, to have sex was to marry that person. Marriage was brought to the home front, legalized by sex. Shortly afterwards, sex was prohibited until marriage, and only when married should one indulge in sex with his or her husband or wife. **There shouldn't be sex until <u>after marriage.</u> This is a hard concept to understand in today's culture.**

We live in a sex-saturated world. Today, everything is sex; TV commercials sell sex, movies, clothing, perfumes, social media, you name it, and even food sells sex. In 1990, I was married as a "make-believer," so was my then-wife. We were both lost. I stated earlier that I was divorced after fourteen years of marriage and then waited another fourteen years to remarry. This time, I was genuinely Born Again by God, not myself. I was saved two weeks after my first divorce, and I studied His Word deeply for 14 years. I have included a poem entitled *(God I thought I Knew)* which explains my conversion *(from Lost to Saved),* which is at the end of this book. When I met my second wife, I knew by this time through God's Word that changing me, His way is the only way. I knew at first sight, once we met, that this was who God wanted for me. We texted online on the website "Christian Mingle" for over a month before meeting. **When the person you prayed about becomes the person you pray with, you recognize God is working.**

It was two months of courting or dating before we even kissed. **She not only prayed with me many times a day, throughout our dating stage, <u>but she also prayed for me!</u>**

I have never witnessed such Christian genuineness in any woman before. She was the real deal. The complete package: a Born Again by God Believer, God-fearing woman, wise, stunningly beautiful, sexy, my very best friend, and she can also make me laugh! The first REAL Christian woman I ever dated. **Obviously, after reading this book, many will say, "I wish this book had been published earlier."** Although I read many books on Christian dating, none explained how to determine whether one is really in the Faith. The other books I read could not pinpoint what to really look for. There were countless books written by those who bought into the lie (free will towards salvation) that anyone can choose Jesus, just by asking Him into one's life. If that were true, they could un-choose Him as well. This is a lie perpetrated by Satan, fooling countless people into *"Easy Believism."* Most Christian dating books are no better than the false books written by those like Joel Osteen or the other countless false teachers out there; line them up.

Satan has hijacked countless pulpits using false "preachers" who push a watered-down *(free-will)* version of the Gospel, which is no Gospel at all. **There were no books available that warned me of what I had experienced in real life, again, thus this book.** When I was dating my wife, she had me read a book she was reading, entitled *"Boundaries"*, which we discussed together. We both even read *"The 5 Love Languages"* before meeting, and we both had the same exact love languages in the same order! We would text each other pictures of the many Christian books we both owned and had read before meeting. We noticed we had several of the same ones! I knew God was orchestrating this final relationship that would lead to our marriage. **All those "relationship" books I** read did nothing to prepare me. **They all fell short in what to look for when considering a Christian spouse.** This book is full of *"straight talk."* There is a time and place for everything. If you require real help in finding that certain person, this is the book. It will teach you how to recognize and confidently identify the real Christian spouse you are truly seeking.

I waited a year of courting her to ask her to marry me; then we had sex <u>after</u> we were married. **We agreed not to have premarital sex, which means both of us are Believers, obeying God.** This was and is essential, and yes, we were both glad we waited. **That way, we would be honoring God through our inactions.** If the woman or man you are dating thinks differently, run! If you both start having sexual relations before marriage, you are both saying that your date is more important than God. It exposes a weakness that develops a lack of trust in each other and in God. Starting or continuing in a relationship that is lustful is NOT of God. You should NOT develop a relationship based on sexual appeal only. I am guilty of doing this earlier in my walk with Jesus, hard lessons, painful ones. This is why and how I know. I regret such huge mistakes; I was rebellious. I sinned against my God. Sin is blinding. I had no real guidance, no real mentor who could smack me awake, Christian to Christian. I didn't have a real book that awakened me to how wrong King Solomon truly was. **I learned that after doing the wrong thing, it is NOT too late to do the right thing**. God does chastise those He loves. Sin has a very high price. All such sinning is against God, cry out for Mercy.

What a Believer needs is truth on how things end up when you color outside the lines of God's wisdom. Certainly, as Believers, we need to seek advice from only other Believers; that's iron sharpens iron. Let's visit **Proverbs 27:17 NKJV** *As iron sharpens iron so a man sharpens the countenance of his friend.* This is why I write for those who need and want correct instruction, Biblically based instruction. **This book can be the iron that sharpens you and deepens your understanding of God's Truths.** When you completely read this book, you will have a much deeper understanding of what you should look for in a spouse. Let's turn to **2 Corinthians 6:14 NKJV** *Do not be unequally yoked together with unbelievers. For what fellowship has righteousness with lawlessness? And what communion has light with darkness?* Here we are instructed to stay away from those who are not like-minded; those who are not Saved. **There can be nothing truthful in common with those still in and of the world.** Dating an unbeliever or a make-believer will be one of your biggest mistakes. This book will provide you with the questions to ask to discern between the lost and Saved.

There was NO book that would teach me what this book sets out to teach. The biggest mistake is having sex before marriage. This should be the old self, not the new self. Christians must refrain from these impulses. When both want to refrain, it's much easier. There are some women who want sex as much as men do. **When a person stands up, declaring sex is only for after marriage, this appears ridiculous to the unsaved and unconverted heart and mind.** When I did find the right woman, the strength was there because we were both like-minded and **equally yoked.** This woman came into my life because of God; it was all His Timing and His Providence. God is in control, and His Timing is perfect. God has a way to make even a crooked arrow hit its mark.

Most women and men are looking for a lustful relationship. They are looking for a *"good time," such as those who* are NOT true believers. This separates true Believers from make-believers. If one could go against God's Word for physical enjoyment, what else would one go against God's Word for? Remember the three main sins are "The Lust of the Eyes, Pride of Life, and The Lust of the Flesh." This leads us to **1 John 2:16 KJV** *For all that is in the world, the lust of the flesh, and the lust of the eyes, and the pride of life, is not of the Father, but is of the world.* The sexual drive is the hardest to overcome. I believe in allowing the four seasons to pass, meaning about one year of courting, even though I am not for long engagements! I am all for accurate examination of one's true Spirit and real character through countless questions, including hands-on Bible study.

If your date won't study God's Word with you each time you ask, run! If, after reading this book **two times** and being as certain as one can be of the other's true conversion by God, while loving the Holy Spirit of God in that person, you get married! **When dating, you should never move in together and do not have premarital sex! Those two actions destroy a person's testimony and reveal a life away from God and His Word.**

Sex is not only for reproduction but for pleasure. Lovemaking is much more than intercourse; it's touching, caressing, exploring every part of each other's body; giving pleasure to each other is God's Gift to married couples. **Proverbs 18:22 NASB** *He who finds a wife finds a good thing and obtains favor from the Lord.* God allows the right person into one's life. This is not always before He allows us to go through many trials, pain, tears, leading to more and more prayer. There are pains from God; He wants us to suffer before He can use us. **God puts His Children through many trials and drops us to where we need to be in front of Him, on our knees!** Also, I would note here that before I was Born Again by God, I belonged to Satan. When I was adopted by God, then I became His Child. When one is Born Again, one is responsible and accountable for adhering to God's Word and removing from one's life what is not pleasing to Him. Let's look at **Proverbs 5:18-19 TLB** *(18) Be happy, yes, rejoice in the wife of your youth. (19) Let her breasts and tender embrace satisfy you. Let her love alone fill you with delight.* Here we see to be happy and rejoice in a wife's love, letting her love ALONE fill you with delight.

Let's visit **Ephesians 5:22-24 NASB** *(22) Wives, subject yourselves to your own husbands, as to the Lord. (23) For the husband is the head of the wife, as Christ also is the head of the church, He Himself being the Savior of the body. (24) But as the church is subject to Christ, so also the wives ought to be to their husbands in everything.* Again, we see God's order in our lives. *The husband is the head of his wife and under God.* We understand God wants the wife to allow her husband to lead and to be in submission to her husband in everything. **God was not being ambiguous here; He is very clear by saying** *everything.* I cannot overstate this Biblical Truth. **I would ask anyone's wife, "If you are not pleasing your own husband, how are you pleasing God?"** Let's visit **Ephesians 5:28 NKJV** *So husbands ought to love their own wives as their own bodies; he who loves his wife loves himself.* A husband must take care of all his wife's needs and desires. No one hates their own body enough to neglect it. These needs and desires include but are not limited to: financial, emotional, physical, Spiritual, and sexual.

Let's go now to **1 Corinthians 7:2-5 NLT** *(2) But because there is so much sexual immorality, each man should have his own wife, and each woman should have her own husband.* God clearly promotes marriage. One reason is because of fornication *(masturbation or pre-marital sex),* which is against God. Sexual immorality includes any sex outside of your own marriage. *(3) The husband should fulfill his wife's sexual needs, and the wife should fulfill her husband's needs. (4) The wife gives authority over her body to her husband, and the husband gives authority over his body to his wife.* **Here, God wants to clear up any confusion as to who owns the other's body.** God says the woman's body belongs to her husband. This means he has full rights to love her as his heart desires. She belongs to him in marriage, surrendering all rights to her whole body to her husband *(only).* This goes both ways.

The husband's body now belongs to his wife *(only)* to love as she wants as well. *(5) Do not deprive each other of sexual relations, unless you both agree to refrain from sexual intimacy for a limited time so you can give yourselves more completely to prayer. Afterward, you should come together again so that Satan won't be able to tempt you because of your lack of self-control.* Here we read that both can agree to a time to not have sex *(such as her menstruation period)* or as in prayer. You see, God in His infinite wisdom also says not to deprive each other. **Understanding sex is more than a want; it's a human need in marriage** *(In many cases, more for the* *husbands*). Your body belongs to your spouse. *When you deprive your spouse of your body, you are being disobedient to God and your spouse.* God wants you both to trust Him; He gave you this man or woman for a short time. He gives you His Love and Himself for all eternity. Time is fleeting; don't waste time arguing about silly things; enjoy one another while you still can.

We should not be limited in our sexual relations with our spouse. The only limitation is that no one else may spoil the marriage bed. **Marriage is an honorable institution, ordained by God. This union that God sanctioned must be kept sexually undefiled or pure from any others.** Today, nothing really goes without saying, so I will say what needs to be said. There is no wife sharing, no threesomes; no one should come between the couple. They should be free to love each other in any way as long as they are both married to each other. Pornography is not okay, but creating your own videos or pictures of each other is okay. It is wise to keep any pictures or videos ONLY between the *husband and wife*. The woman should allow her husband to do what he pleases to satisfy his desires for her. The man should do as his wife asks to please her desires as well.

The goal in a good marriage is to make your spouse happy. **Fulfilling each other's marital obligations sexually can be a challenge.** Remember, there is a difference between your spouse telling you what he or she wants and your spouse doing what he or she wants. Sex should be agreed upon happily by both. The things you both agreed on before marriage should be adhered to. What's needed is for you both to work on a solution you both agree on. Remembering to love, it's now **1**

Peter 4:8 KJV *And above all things have fervent charity among yourselves: for charity shall cover the multitude of sins.* There are other versions of the Bible that say "LOVE," but <u>charity</u> is the highest form of love; the *King James Version* is spot on here. A Christian's love should never be arrogant, selfish, or sarcastic; those are traits of Satan, not God. It's never his way or her way or the highway. You should take your qualms to God's Word, not to your family, neighbor, or friends. Don't allow others to tell you what's normal. Remember, *"normal"* is a cycle on a washing machine. Normal does not describe a Christian. There will always be reasons not to please the other and to <u>compromise</u>. Focus on the reasons why you should please your spouse. God's Word is clear on this turn to **1 Corinthians 7:4 ESV** *For the wife does not have authority over her own body, but the husband does. Likewise, the husband does not have authority over his own body, but the wife does.* You should both go all-out to enjoy sex, pleasing each other.

This means sexual toys are okay. Countless sexual positions are okay, dressing up or dressing down is okay. Playing games with each other is all okay. If you're a woman and your husband wants you to walk around the house with almost nothing on, or nothing on, why argue? She should just do as he would like. This, of course, goes both ways. There is an old saying for women, *"Dress and act like a lady when going out, be a great cook in the kitchen, and dress and act like a whore in the bedroom."* If that pleases your husband, why not do it? Let's make sure there are no kids around; remember, two are now one. The sex you both share at times should include eye-to-eye contact; it should be very intimate. The man should always cherish his wife, understand her needs, and listen to her requests. She should trust him and feel fully protected by him. Both of you should work towards losing all inhibitions and reaching a higher level of intimacy that few ever attain. **Sex for married couples is God's Gift of entertainment, fun, and excitement.** It's the most enjoyment God's Children will encounter until we arrive in Heaven.

Let's say you create a game as a *"merit system."* Where, if he or she does this or that, you will do this or that, or do as he or she wants. *Remember, this is only a game.* Our real life should never consist of a merit system. There are no ultimatums concerning marital sex. Sex is not to be negotiated unless it's for a *"game scenario."* Both of you could agree to this for a limited time only. If your body belongs to your spouse, you cannot *negotiate what already belongs to them.* Although negotiations are always intensified when you make heartfelt requests rather than harsh demands. **Tell each other you love him or her! When a couple has great sex than you know he or she adores you!** Great sex is not only physical but emotional and vocal as well; say the things your heart feels. Try using a blind fold; try things that may stimulate the other. If your woman or man wants to hear you say certain things which excite him or her, say them. It is important that our words pertain only to each other. The things you both may have talked about before marriage should be acted out now. Try sexual things you both always wanted to try; this is the time. The best marriages are those where both spouses are not afraid to say what they feel. Their love and passion should be open and obvious towards each other. **Some couples would rather die than please each other, while a Christian couple would die to please each other; see the difference?**

Sex must be between the two of you, husband and wife, man and woman. There is nothing but great joy in bringing each other to a loud, vociferous climax. Both should feel unrestricted and totally open to experimenting with each other in ways reserved only for their marriage. A couple should feel permitted to achieve sexual ecstasy, use their imagination, and enjoy! **God created sex ONLY for marriage.** Rejoice in this fact, expand your limitations, and make your spouse very, very happy. Talk together about what would make you sad or deprived. Don't let your spouse feel deprived; give him or her more than enough love and sex. Let his or her cup run over with ecstasy! Let each other know your inner thoughts. Be completely open and honest with each other. Great sex is a work in progress…

If you both think of pleasing the other, then it's a win-win, but if one is selfish in love-making, you will both lose. A couple should put aside a time, as in a session, to have sex; turn off the phones, lock the door, and turn off the television. Together, focus on pleasing the other person in their fantasies as long as it's regarding the two of you. Sometimes being spontaneous is adventurous. It is fun to be spontaneous without rigid limitations. There are no sexual restrictions between you both. Although many may "think this or that" about you if you were to reveal your bedroom antics or play with anyone, don't. I would advise you never to reveal to anyone what you do together as a married couple in your bedroom, kitchen, vehicle, or anywhere else. This should only be between the two of you. This would be the only way to assure each other of your marital privacy. Remember, your sex life is NOT for public display.

If one of you "kiss and tell," the other will never feel unrestricted enough to open up to their private sensual wants or needs. That will therefore limit your full sexual desires within your marriage, and that is a sad situation to be in. We should be free sexually amongst each other, which is a joy. This goes back to the Garden before sin, with Adam and Eve. Feel free to open up to each other and respect each other. It is important to promise one another assurance and confidence to never divulge the full extent of each other's lovemaking to anyone else, period. Talk openly about what turns you on and vice versa. **Sex is the glue that keeps good marriages together.** Enjoy and have sex as often as either one wants. Then there's never a worry or concern that the other will cheat or fantasize about another but you. If you fulfill all of his or her fantasies, you are truly in love with your spouse. In marriage, each should seek to be more thoughtful and understanding of their spouse's sexual requests, creating a bond that grows closer. This gives each other confidence and a level of intimacy few ever achieve, but all want. Don't forget date night; set a night (once a week, or more often) to get out and date each other! Take walks together, work out together; never forget you are each other's best friend. The dating process should never end. Christian men all want a Godly woman. Let's jump to **Proverbs 31:10-13 NKJV** and break it down slowly… *(10) Who can find a virtuous wife? For her worth is far above rubies.* Here we see a woman who is Godly, capable, intelligent, and honest with morals. Finding a woman like this is priceless. God would have to intercede and arrange for her to marry the right man. **This type of woman is a <u>prize</u> to her husband, which translates to <u>exceptionally desirable</u>.**

(11) The heart of her husband safely trusts her; so he will have no lack of gain. The husband of such a woman has nothing to worry about because she is above reproach. He would have secure confidence in her loyalty to him.

(12) She does him good and not evil all the days of her life. She will encourage her husband, building him up and never breaking him down, never belittling him. She is always a complete helpmate and a comfort to him. She would never speak loudly to him in public. She would never be an embarrassment to him at any time, but a joy.

(13) She seeks wool and flax, and willingly works with her hands. Here is a woman not afraid to get her hands dirty or break a fingernail, willing to work with and alongside her husband.

Jump to **Proverbs 31:17 NKJV** *She girds herself with strength, And strengthens her arms.* We see here that she *physically works out,* taking care of her Temple *(body)* to be fit for any God-given task. Let's look at **Proverbs 31:26 NKJV** *She opens her mouth with wisdom, And on her tongue is the law of kindness.* We notice here that she is skillful, kind, and guided by Godly Wisdom; she is **able to counsel, instruct, and correct other women, including children, concerning Biblical Truths.** *See my wife's book on page 174*

Let's now take a look at **Proverb 31:30 NKJV** *Charm is deceitful and beauty is passing, but a woman who fears the Lord, she shall be praised.* Here in Proverbs 31, God's Word is identifying a TRUE woman of God. **Every True Believer needs to marry a woman who fears God.** A woman who obeys and worships The Lord reverently and puts her trust in God's Holy

Word each day. This is the type of woman a man of God seeks. I would suggest that if you do not find one, keep searching. **I searched for fourteen years to find one.** These women are rare, but God will provide a Proverbs 31 woman to those who are willing to serve and live for Him. I do believe that. We know God feeds the birds, and they diligently seek their food. They don't just wake up and open their beak, and food falls in. They must go and find food.

The Christian should not hide in their closet and pray for God to bring someone to their door. The Christian man must seek to find a Christian wife. <u>The seeker should always be the man</u>. Therefore, a single Christian woman needs to make herself somewhat visible, even by meeting at the gym or on a CHRISTIAN dating site, as we did!

Chapter 7

Homosexuality

Homosexuality is NOT of God. It's a sad matter that I must explain; that a life of homosexuality is un-Godly and NOT accepted by God in any way. There is no such thing as marriage between a woman and a woman or a man and a man; this is sexual perversion, and God calls such an **Abomination**. Let's look at **Genesis 19:1-14 NASB,** breaking it down slowly…

(1) Now the two angels came to Sodom in the evening as Lot was sitting at the gate of Sodom. When Lot saw them, he stood up to meet them and bowed down with his face to the ground. Here we see two Angels *(who are always men; there are no woman, Angels; period).* Lot, showed them humility and great respect.

(2) And he said, "Now behold, my lords, please turn aside into your servant's house, and spend the night, and wash your feet; then you may rise early and go on your way." They said, "No, but we shall spend the night in the public square." We notice here that the appearance of the Angels was that of normal men *(no wings).*

(3) Yet he strongly urged them, so they turned aside to him and entered his house; and he prepared a feast for them and baked unleavened bread, and they ate. We can also notice that the two Angelic Beings were able to eat food as we do.

(4) Before they lay down, the men of the city—the men of Sodom—surrounded the house, both young and old, all the

people from every quarter; **Here we see the wicked and evil perversions of the gay lifestyle lived out, without restraint.**

(5) and they called to Lot and said to him, "Where are the men who came to you tonight? Bring them out to us that we may have relations with them." We can clearly see the true intentions of those men living in the cities of Sodom & Gomorrah. They wanted to have sex with the two men visitors, who, unbeknownst to those outside Lot's home, were indeed two Angels.

(6) But Lot went out to them at the doorway, and shut the door behind him, (7) and said, "Please, my brothers, do not act wickedly. (8) Now look, I have two daughters who have not had relations with any man; please let me bring them out to you, and do to them whatever you like; only do not do anything to these men, because they have come under the shelter of my roof." (9) But they said, "Get out of the way!" They also said, "This one came in as a foreigner, and already he is acting like a judge; now we will treat you worse than them!" So they pressed hard against Lot and moved forward to break the door. (10) But the men reached out their hands and brought Lot into the house with them, and shut the door. (11) Then they struck the men who were at the doorway of the house with blindness, from the small to the great, so that they became weary of trying to find the doorway. Here we read that Lot offered his two virgin daughters to appease the mob outside. The mob was threatening, unruly, and out for male-to-male gay sex only. This was why God sent the two Angels to get Lot and then to destroy the two cities. Lot had no understanding of how powerful Angels are. The Angels blinded the men outside so they would go away.

(12) Then the two men (Angels) said to Lot, "Whom else do you have here? A son-in-law and your sons and daughters, and whomever you have in the city, bring them out of the place; (13) for we are about to destroy this place, because their outcry has become so great before the Lord that the Lord has sent us to destroy it." (14) So Lot went out and spoke to his sons-in-law, who were to marry his daughters, and said, "Up, get out of this place, for the Lord is destroying the city." But he appeared to his sons-in-law to be joking. We see here that the two Angels gave Lot a last opportunity to remove anyone else, including his two potential sons-in-law, who did not take Lot seriously. **That reminds me of Noah's Ark, so few take God seriously.** Today, we have the completed Word of God, yet few even care or take it seriously...

(24) Then the Lord rained brimstone and fire on Sodom and Gomorrah from the Lord out of heaven, (25) and He overthrew those cities, and all the surrounding area and all the inhabitants of the cities, and what grew on the ground. (26) But Lot's wife, from behind him, looked back, and she became a pillar of salt. Here are the two cities at the end: Sodom and Gomorrah. **God totally destroyed them and the evil sexual perversions of the homosexuals. The gay lifestyle is an Abomination to the Lord.** God has shown us such mercy after the flood. Today, God would wipe California, New York, and Chicago clear off the map! **We also see that Lot's wife could not even follow the simple instruction not to look back.**

Let's see what happens to such people as those who are homosexuals, it's **Revelation 21:8 NASB** *(8) But for the cowardly, and unbelieving, and abominable, and murderers,* *and sexually immoral persons, and sorcerers, and idolaters, and all liars, their part will be in the lake that burns with fire and brimstone, which is the second death.*" Here we read those who do not confess freely Jesus as GOD and boldly defend God's Word; they are on this list. It includes those who do not believe in Jesus as the only way for their salvation, the only path to Heaven. We see that those who murder, which would include those who hate and those who condone abortion. We see that sexual immorality, as in the gay lifestyle, is an Abomination and is not accepted. We see that those who partake in astrology or witchcraft, black magic, Ouija boards, cults, and false religions are not accepted. **We see that those who buy into lying; it does say ALL liars. It goes on to expose just what their eternity will be, which is Hell.**

Let's look at **Leviticus 18:22 GNT** *No man is to have sexual relations with another man; God hates that.* **This is as clear as it gets.** God says it's the worst of the worst of sins. Now jump to **Deuteronomy 22:5 NASB** *"A woman shall not wear a man's clothing, nor shall a man put on a woman's clothing; for whoever does these things is an abomination to the Lord your God.* **Here, this would include those who claim to be transvestites, cross-dressers, or those who think it's funny, as in those in movies or shows.** There are many Hollywood-type Godless fools like Eddie Murphy, Martin Lawrence, Jamie Foxx, Robin Williams, Marlon & Shawn Wayans, Tyler Perry, and others who felt it was okay, even funny, to publicly act out such an *Abomination.* Let's jump to **1 Corinthians 6:9-11 NASB** *(9) Or do you not know that the unrighteous will not inherit the kingdom of God? Do not be deceived; neither the sexually immoral, nor idolaters, nor adulterers, **nor***

98

homosexuals, (10) nor thieves, nor the greedy, nor those habitually drunk, nor verbal abusers, nor swindlers, will inherit the kingdom of God. (11) Such were some of you; but you were washed, but you were sanctified, but you were justified in the name of the Lord Jesus Christ and in the Spirit of our God.

Those who think this is funny, it's definitely not! It's shameful, and God is disgusted with and at them. They will all end up in Hell. **Paul goes on to say that some of us were such, but once saved by God, not ourselves, we are totally changed.** A Born Again Believer would never cross-dress or relate to the list above except in the past tense. God uses the list above to explain in detail who will be thrown into Hell. When someone is Saved, they repent from those evil sins above and wholeheartedly believe in Jesus. This transformation is only possible for those God chooses to be His Adopted Children. **There are many who say in word only, they love the Lord like that fool, Tyler Perry, who made over seven cross-dressing movies!** These frauds of the faith are easy to spot *(see chapter 4 "Identify a Born Again Believer").* **Money drives people to do whatever Satan would have them do, but God will not be mocked.** This points to **Psalm 36:2 NIV** *In their own eyes they flatter themselves too much to detect or hate their sin.* This exposes all of Hollywood's celebrities and the many around the world who love them.

I will quote R.C. Sproul, *"My experience as an Apologist and Minister has shown me that the real reason most people reject Christianity is not for lack of evidence. The proof from external sources regarding the Truth of the Biblical account is too overwhelming. No, the real issue is a MORAL ONE."*

I agree. The world simply loves its sin much more than its love for the God of the Bible.

When your love for God's Truths outweighs your fear of offending someone, you've arrived at where God is Pleased.

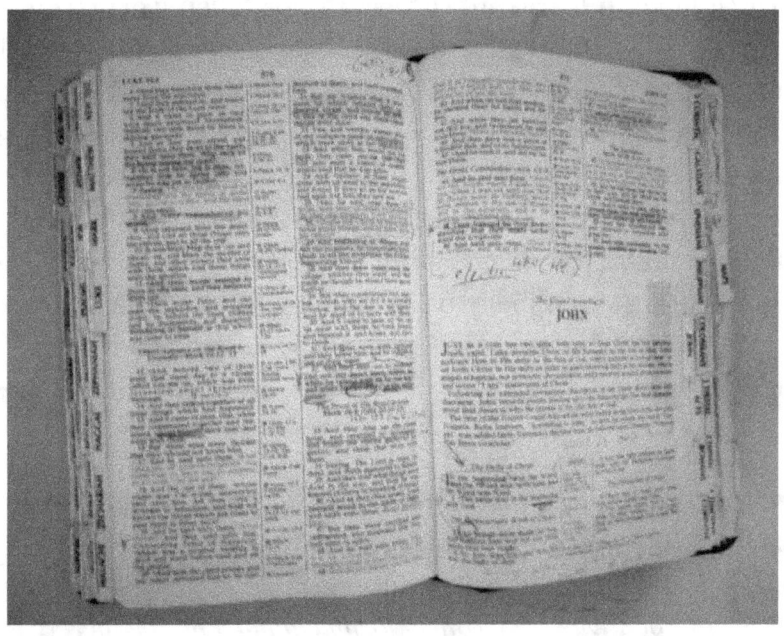

You CAN NOT love JESUS unless YOU love to bathe in

HIS WORD

Chapter 8

Marital Leadership

First, to open this topic, you would have to realize that God's Word is prominent in the lives of both husband and wife. **We must place God first in marriage, or it's not under His Protection and Care, but subject to this fallen world.** If your marriage is worldly, there is a fifty-fifty chance of divorce. If you are both **TRUE** Born Again Believers, you will both happily want to obey God's Word, knowing that doing so pleases God. There will be VERY little to ZERO chance of divorce. **What's lacking in most Christian men today is Biblical maturity;** *(leadership)* **most are stuck in Biblical infancy.** Most men today want to be babied by their wives as they were by their own mothers. They do not lead their wives as God instructs.

Let's visit **1 Peter 3:1-9 NASB** *(1).. you wives, be subject to your own husbands so that even if any of them are disobedient to the word, they may be won over without a word by the behavior of their wives, (2) as they observe your pure and respectful behavior. (3) Your adornment must not be merely the external—braiding the hair, wearing gold jewelry, or putting on apparel;* let's break down these three verses. We see here that if one marries and then finds out their husband is not a true believer, an obedient woman (wife) may be used by God to open their eyes *(it goes both ways)*. This is why I stress that **before** you get married, be certain he or she is a **REAL BELIEVER**. **The book** *"Digging Deeper into God's Truth Defines a Christian"* **is a book you both should read together.** If you read the Word of God without truly understanding scripture, there is no real value. It's important to fully understand that the scripture is of ALL value. I use the Bible to interrupt the Bible. Get that book! **Please make sure you both understand and fully agree on what a TRUE Christian is.** The second and third verse here indicates that your behavior as a wife should be pure and respectful. It says your adornment must not merely be external. A person's looks are not only external, suggesting that they do play a part. Dress to impress your husband or wife in any type of apparel that he or she may like to see you in. What's more important than that? Show him or her your LOVE. **Remember, you do not need permission to do what's right in God's Eyes.**

Let's move on to verse *(4) but it should be the hidden person of the heart, with the imperishable quality of a gentle and quiet spirit, which is precious in the sight of God. (5) For in this way the holy women of former times, who hoped in God, also used to adorn themselves, being subject to their own husbands, (6) just as Sarah obeyed Abraham, **calling him lord;** and you have proved to be her children if you do what is right without being frightened by any fear.* **There are many women who will run from the above verses, but women of God will run to them.** Men love the heart of a true Christian woman because of their quiet, kind, and gentle spirit. This pleases God greatly. **A loud or clamorous woman dishonors her husband.** The sixth verse here is a hard pill to swallow for the world; they hate it. *The true woman of God always shows deep respect and honor for her husband.* It is a Blessing to have a Godly wife who is in full agreement with God's Word. She is not afraid of what her lost friends or lost family members may think or say.

Remember, we are not of this world, but are saved by God to think and act very differently.

Let's go to verse *(7) You husbands in the same way, live with your wife in an understanding way, as with someone weaker, since she is a woman; and show her honor as a fellow heir of the grace of life, so that your prayers will not be hindered.* This verse tells husbands that a wife is not a plaything but an equal person in Christ. **She must be treated with tender understanding, love, and honor, placing her before everything and everyone in the world but God.** When you do this, it allows God to better hear and want to hear your prayers. Meekness is power under control; be tender and kind with your wife. **I believe kindness on both sides is a must for any relationship to work; be kind.**

Let's look at verse *(8) To sum up, all of you be harmonious, sympathetic, loving, compassionate, and humble; (9) not returning evil for evil or insult for insult, but giving a blessing instead; for you were called for the very purpose that you would inherit a blessing.* Here, we see that God wants us to be loving, caring, and to show true compassion. **Never fight with each other using ANY demeaning, vulgar, harsh, cruel words or pushing, grabbing, or hitting; NEVER!** Remember, you are both blessed to be a blessing to each other and other people. Look at it this way: **each of you is a gift from God to the other.** In marriage, each is a priceless gift to be cared for. Both should seek ways to bless and edify each other in a tender and exclusive way. **Learn to lift each other up in love, with God as the Father of you both.** He is the source of all blessings.

This way, you both are setting an example of a Godly Marriage to the lost world.

I remember a short story that is packed with Biblical meaning. The husband asked his wife how much money she had. Well, she told him and happily gave him all she had. He then decided to purchase a small potato farm in Idaho. He invested all the money in that farm, and in a short time, they were going broke, so he sold it before losing everything. He had another idea: to start a small business, and she followed his lead, but that, too, lost money. They both soon had nothing left and lived in a tent. He said he loved her deeply, and she said she did as well, adding, "I will happily follow your lead regardless of where that goes, for I am your loving wife." There was no "love gets funny when there is no money." This example may seem extreme to most, but such scenarios happen every day. It does not always mean the business plan was wrong; *I personally lost everything I owned during the 2008 economic downturn. There was a time I lived in my vehicle.* In this story, this man's wife was considerate, loving, and respectful, devoted, and always by her husband's side, as God would want. **This is an example of a woman of God. Regardless of money, that is a marriage blessed by God.**

This is a very common scenario: let's say a man repeatedly asks his wife to dress a certain way at home. She hears him and understands what he wants, but she does not accommodate him. It can be as simple as a request to wear an outfit he purchased for her, but she doesn't even bother to hear him out or try it on. What she is doing is belittling his simple desires. She is not giving in to her husband's request, because she chooses not to accommodate him; it may be inconvenient in her view. If such a pattern develops as simple as his request was, or maybe it disrupts their marriage. Place enough unanswered requests back-to-back (doesn't matter what they're about), and their communication bond is significantly severed; it goes both ways. If a relationship continues on this twisted path of neglecting a spouse's request, as in not meeting his or her wishes, there is a marital disconnect.

This scenario, of course, goes both ways. This damage often manifests as resentment toward the other. The act of NOT wanting to please the husband or wife is a sin. It is wise to allow the other to enjoy his or her little fantasies. If they involve one another within the marriage, why should there be any disconnect? When you both are happily indulging in each other's playful desires, it keeps the marriage stimulating. Accommodating your spouse's requests may just excite you as well; go for it! Work out these little issues so they never become big issues later. *Listen to each other's voices over all other voices.*

Remember, Abraham's wife Sara addressed her husband as Lord. Biblical respect from a wife towards her husband today is rare; even repulsive to those who are lost. God's Truths have been greatly distorted for the sake of popularity.

Again, sex is like the glue that holds a marriage together. Sexual attraction is important, yet what one finds sexy in their mate, others may not. Beauty or attractions are solely in the eye of the beholder. Whatever turns on each spouse about the other during the dating stage will last throughout their marriage, regardless of age. This is why older people always find their spouses attractive, regardless of age. They continue having sex in their nineties and some beyond. Love is in the heart and soul of those saved by God. His Love is everlasting in them. Saved couples see past the skin, past the sex, and into eternity. Feed into what your partner wants, desires, and requests. Then there will be an overflow of good sex in your lives. Treat each other like royalty; go that extra mile to please them. **Your wife may want you to help clean the house; to her, that could be foreplay.** Try to please each other in the little things. This will lead to complete satisfaction in other areas as well.

Don't fall into the trap of not supplying your spouse with what he or she requires sexually, as long as he or she has told you what those desires are. This should be discussed before marriage. This way, it does not come as a surprise but as a subject of candid concern. If there is no agreement between the two, there may be a <u>compromise</u>. Talk all things out together. When you don't bring up certain private concerns **before** marriage, they may lead to a disaster while married. It's imperative that you both make an agreement and or compromise together, or a door may open as in acting out his or her fantasies with another. We should avoid a situation like King David's. If you are not interested in the amount of sex or type of sex your spouse may request, indulge her or him *(make an attempt)* anyway; you're married. You may learn to like it, grow to like it, or simply do whatever to satisfy her or him because of your true love. This, of course, must go both ways. The old saying is "What's good for the goose is good for the gander." This exposes your real desire to please your spouse. The yearning and desire to please each other must be much stronger than your reasoning to not please him or her. **Although there will be days or moments when one is not in the mood or having a bad day**. This is why communication is vital. We should always be kind and understanding towards one another.

Remember, this is the man or woman you selected and vowed to God to be with forever, "until death do you part." It's not wise to displease your spouse. The power to please the other is in your mind. **Your actions will speak volumes.** You both should try to accomplish each other's passions because of love. It may take some time to get to the point where you see this. When we examine why some do not go that extra mile to please their spouse, we find they are selfish reasons.

True Love is based on charity, and it may take a lot of charity to succumb to one's desires. This is a good thing, not a bad thing. Look at it this way: he or she wants you so much as to expose his or her deepest desires to you and for you. When married, we aim to please our spouse, not demean them. Most times, it's best to simply go that extra step, doing whatever it may take to please him or her. It's well worth doing all you can, without hesitation or saying no. The word "NO" itself turns off your spouse; sometimes, such is irreversible and becomes a mental block while trying to get aroused sexually. However, hearing the word "no" is the risk one takes. When letting their guard down is to reveal sexually what one may honestly expect from the other. Many couples today think little about genuinely making their spouse sexually happy, and not even caring has sadly become today's norm. This has weakened and destroyed the integrity of most marriages. **The True Christian marriage**

allows mercy and displays grace. Let's remember, Satan came to steal, kill, and destroy; don't allow him any leverage in your relationship.

Let's look at **1 Corinthians 11:3 NKJV** *(3) But I want you to know that the head of every man is Christ, the head of woman is man, and the head of Christ is God.* Let's dig deeper than most on this verse. **This verse, of course, means a husband over his own wife.** This would include their home, kids, financial affairs, sexual concerns, and decisions of all types. **This also bleeds into Church and politics. There should be no women who are allowed to lead cities or states, such as governors or Mayors. This same command from God would include Congress, the Senate, or the Presidency. The Godless liberal Feminist movement** is one reason we see the decline of America and in other Nations. Anarchy ensues because of the decline of listening to and obeying God's Holy Word. This deterioration begins with a loss of morality and, consequently, leads to total disrespect for God's Word. The feminist movement has become the norm. **The feminist movement is from Satan, such is totally against the Word of God.** There are some "churches" that think it's okay, saying times have changed and now women can even preach! This is yet another Abomination. God is the same yesterday, today, and tomorrow. He will not be mocked; there is a huge price to pay for such disobedience.

Let's jump over to **1 Timothy 2:11-14 ESV** *(11) Let a woman learn quietly with all submissiveness. (12) I do not permit a woman to teach or to exercise authority over a man; rather, she is to remain quiet. (13) For Adam was formed first,* *then Eve; (14) and Adam was not deceived, but the <u>woman was</u> <u>deceived</u> and became a transgressor.* There are many today who believe God was joking here, in trying to twist scripture to think a woman can preach. **A woman can teach children and other women, but never men. They cannot be a Preacher.** Those who think they can teach men are simply false teachers, false converts. Their pride is in the world. They are disrespecting and abusing God's Word; such are the lost. These women are deceiving countless baby Christians and, in doing so, will reap deadly rewards. Jump over to **1 Corinthians 14:34-35 NIV** *(34) Women should remain silent in the churches. They are not allowed to speak, but must be in submission, as the law says. (35) If they want to inquire about something, they should ask their own husbands at home; for it is disgraceful for a woman to speak in the church.* This verse is more than enough to illustrate that a woman must never preach. God calls it disgraceful, and false teachers don't care. **A "church" that would allow a woman to preach or teach men is a "church" under Satan's rule, not God's.** Women should ask their husbands for Biblical wisdom. And he should live in God's Word and be able to answer her questions.

Therefore, I stress that both the husband and the wife need to study God's Word diligently each and every day. Reading through the whole Bible, not just parts you may like. In addition to my own daily Bible studies (sometimes eight hours a day while writing), my wife and I have taken over two and a half years to completely read and study through the whole Bible together. We are continually reading it from Genesis to Revelation. We read and study one to four chapters each day. This practice has brought us much closer together in our marriage and in Christ. This practice continues each day and will continue until Jesus comes or takes us Home. When one is Born Again by God, they understand, love, and obey the Scriptures together. **Christians find God's Word not only interesting and insightful but spiritually and eternally rewarding.** The Bible never gets old. Every time I read it, it enlightens me and teaches me more and more. I thank God for His Mercy and His Grace countless times each day.

We warrant a Godless condition of lawlessness and disorder when we collectively turn our backs on God. Placing women over men is an abomination unto the Lord. **It was never His Way, but for unlearned and wicked men and stubborn Godless women.** This has happened because God's Word has been removed from schools, politics, households, and "churches." I have frequented countless "churches" over the past twenty years, only to find very few, if any, address this concern. **There are many, many "churches" today that are dead, using false teachers preaching to false converts looking to have their ears tickled.** Truth is the new lie for many.

Let's look at **1 Corinthians 11:8-9 NKJV** *(8) For man is not from woman, but woman from man. (9) Nor was man created for the woman, but woman for the man.* Here we plainly see the order of God's Intent. Let's jump back again to **Genesis 2:18 NASB** *(18) Then the Lord God said, "It is not good for the man to be alone; I will make him a helper suitable for him."* We understand here the order and origin of women. God made woman as a helpmate for man, not the other way around. **Christian men want a woman who will edify him, not crucify him.** Biblically, there were never any queens whom God used to conquer land or lead their armies to victory. **God never chose any woman to lead an Army or to be a Prophet, a King, a Pastor or an Apostle.** Yes, there were women in the Bible God used, mainly because there were no men, man enough to take charge, at that particular time. **There were also women like** *Delilah* **and** *Jezebel,* **who God allowed to destroy men because of men's weakness.** Give a read to this Poem entitled simply, "Jezebel," taken from the book *"God's Clarity through Poetry 2."*

Jezebel

Do you know a contentious woman? Are you one? Did you marry one? Are you dating one? In the beginning, they seem to look so pretty and to be so much fun, but once identified, if not married...RUN, YES RUN!

The tongue has the power of life and death; she uses hers to control your soul...to you, I say woe!

They are likely to cause and provoke an argument, they're quick-tempered, they are out to embarrass, control, manipulate...to steal, kill, and destroy...

They have a short fuse, and they're out to abuse! At first it's hard to tell, but you just might be dating or married to a Jezebel...

Yes, God's Word says it best...says it well... "It is better to dwell in the wilderness than be with a contentious and angry woman."... "A quarrelsome wife is like a constant dripping on a rainy day." ... "Restraining her is like restraining the wind or grasping oil with your hand."... "It's better to live in a corner of a roof than in a house shared with a contentious woman."

These are all God's Words...His advice... It's firm, and we must learn; His counsel is not shallow or hollow...and it's easy to follow...

A contentious woman does not listen....she must lead, and constantly talks back...is stubborn, self-righteous, and too proud, and is always...much too loud...

The contentious do not obey truth, but obey unrighteousness, anger, and wrath...before you date, do the math...

If she talks too loud, she'll embarrass you in a crowd...if she likes to swear, scheme, scream, thinks she's a man's dream...run, she's on the wrong team...

She'll have little submission and no accountability...all about her control and her vanity...and she'll complain, nag, be non-supportive to her man...just run far, far away, as fast, fast as you can...

She'll argue, always pointing her finger at her man...but never at herself...no fruit of being saved at all...didn't hear God's Effectual Call but His External call, that's all...she'll cause a good man, yes, a Godly man to fall and fall and fall...

But right now, it still may be your call...If she doesn't let you lead, she'll make your heart bleed...She'll always stir up strife, so don't make her your wife...

Run to save your very, very own life.

The Jezebel woman is full of rebellion, disrespect...her pride won't hide...honesty and modesty not there...And in God, have no fear...

Such are un-teachable, if God's Truth doesn't line up with their opinion, will speak loud, shout, curse and talk over you, as to give you an order...

Believe me, such a woman can only lead you to spiritual slaughter and a mental disorder...

She does a dishonor to her man...Many claim to be "Christian"...full of unaddressed sin...and so controlling within...

won't sit and study God's Word with you...for such a heart is not sincere or true, not a heart you would want to win...Please, don't give in...

She would rather throw your sins in your face, while they are hers as well, but she doesn't see that, can't tell...

There's a log in her eye while she condemns the speck in yours...

If she won't initiate Bible Study... find another woman buddy...

Look rather for a Proverbs 31 woman and rejoice...she will demand no sex before marriage, wait to marry you, and you'll wait and want her too...

She'll respect you, look up to you, and as Sara called her husband Abraham, Lord, with such respect, you both will be in one accord...

For with her you will find soft, kind words, wisdom, happiness, honor, edification, and a blessed life...that's the one you want...a God-picked wife...

Placing Christ first in all you both do is key, believe me...if you don't...finding God's Peace, you will have little to no chance; you'll merely stumble into a regrettable worldly romance, remember, a three-strand cord is not easily broken...

Don't use God as a mere token...

You want to help a contentious woman?...well YOU can't...only God through Christ can...if she totally surrenders her life to Him...and looks deep within...a mirror is needed...

God's Word nor wisdom cannot be superseded...she must humble herself, cry out for His Mercy...confess, recognize, repent, admitting all of her wrongdoing...placing

Christ first, He alone is worth pursuing...He alone opens closed eyes and renews hearts...

JOSEPH MALARA

A Christian man must go through Christ to reach her, and then that's worth doing...

No-one but Christ can change a life...no one else can really help a contentious at all...run and pray...then it's God's Call...

If you're not equally yoked...if she doesn't edify you, if she's not your motivator but your criticizer, if she's sarcastic, a provoker, instigator, a joker, antagonizer...

no one but Christ can make her wiser...don't despise her...

Introduce and reintroduce Christ into her life...if she doesn't transform, just speak truth into her life, but never ever make her your wife...

if you see no Godly Change it's a NO...so please fast, let her go...

Remember, you cannot help her at all...the more you try, the more you both will fall...

You will do less and less for Christ, and soon nothing, nothing, and nothing at all...leading to a Godless life...

When you finally identify a contentious woman...it matters little, how long you have been seeing each other...that's just a deeper hole you keep digging, my Brother...

It's best to just leave her alone...she'll only bring you down, she'll bring you great pain, drive you insane, yes you'll moan...and in Christ never be fully grown...

And there goes your dream of a happy, happy home...

Leave the contentious woman alone...to what she within herself has sown...

But, if you marry one, she's your very, very own Jezebel...till death do you part...

so remember while dating, please first guard your heart...

God Says To Be Wise...

And Don't Be Fooled By Those Pretty, Pretty Eyes!

Revelation 2:20-23 MSG *"But why do you let that Jezebel who calls herself a prophet mislead my dear servants into Cross-denying, self-indulging religion? I gave her a chance to change her ways, but she has no intention of giving up a career in the god-business. I'm about to lay her low, along with her partners, as they play their sex-and-religion games. The bastard offspring of their idol-whoring, I'll kill. Then every church will know that appearances don't impress me. I x-ray every motive and make sure you get what's coming to you."*

THE

JEZEBEL

SPIRIT

Chapter 9

Three Umbrella Rule

Let's use a *Three Umbrella Rule* to simplify and explain the role of a **Christian** Marriage. **Let's examine, under the top umbrella is Christ** (who educates, authorizes, and guides the husband). **Let's examine, under the second umbrella, the HUSBAND** (defends, provides for the family, accomplishes the will of God). **Let's examine, under the third umbrella, the wife (who wants to serve her husband (helpmate) with Joy, takes care of children if any, oversees the household, and** is kind and humble). **This is the <u>correct order, and Jesus is Lord and leads</u>.** This brings a blessed life: obeying God's Will through His Word is **doing Right by God and *Living in His Spiritual LIGHT!***

Let's use a *Three Umbrella Rule* to explain the role of a *Worldly* **Marriage. Let's examine, under the top umbrella, is Satan,** who uses the Godless liberal ideology (perverts and undermines the family). **Let's examine, under the second umbrella, the WIFE** (allows Satan access to the children, if any, disempowers and controls the husband). **Let's examine, under the third umbrella, the Husband** (household in disorder, man's purpose is demoralized and rejected; the will of God is unfulfilled).

This is the <u>incorrect</u> order, and Satan is the lord and has the lead. This brings confusion and chaos. Disobeying God's Will does NOT bring a blessed life. **This is to love the world, which is** *doing right by Satan, living in his spiritual DARKNESS!*

Chapter 10

Relationship Communication

Communication starts by telling the truth. Real life is full of hard issues. We must learn how to deal with them Biblically. Establish your foundation on the Lord. Run to God's Word for instruction. **We should always run to God's Word for counsel and look to Jesus for strength and guidance.** There was a time when I was going through a very hard time of separation before divorce. My ex-wife went to a mutual friend *(from the old Pentecostal "church" we attended)* as a mediator to talk with and offer his advice. The advice he gave us both was simply to look towards "damage control." This type of wicked counsel is of Satan, not God. It was the blind leading the blind. **It is important to make sure you are never influenced by people who are not influenced by God.** The point I am making here is simply that the wrong advice from the lost world only leads **to more and more wrong.**

My ex-wife also went to her woman friends, who were also lost, and they told her to *"grab all you can,"* so she stole money from funds that belonged to us both and even funds that belonged to others! She hired a lawyer and went after things I didn't even own. She was not at all interested in reconciliation but a fresh start with newfound money and a new man. **Thank God, I hold no resentment. Resentment is anger gone underground. God wants His Children to forgive and move on.** My ex-wife never sat down with me to explain what, how, and why certain things happened in our then-14-year marriage; there was gossip about a small issue. I immediately said to her,

"Let's sit down in my office and talk." Instead, she ran to the bank and elsewhere, looking to capitalize on foolish gossip. We never talked it out. She was cold, using any setback as an excuse to run, which only made the worst-case scenario worse. **The tree of non-communication has its roots in confusion.** This is all from and of this world; by communicating with *foolish people* in place of the One whom we really need, God. But we did not know Him…Thus, this book!

When a couple is married, and neither party wants to talk, that relationship needs Christian counseling, not separation. This is when you MUST TALK, NOT RUN. **The time to run is BEFORE you get married, not after.** There should be real Biblical communication and truth, not speculation. If your spouse or the person you're dating will NOT even talk with you face-to-face about matters affecting the relationship, then that person will definitely create a false narrative about you behind your back. **Marriage is the making of a vow, a Holy Covenant with each other and with God. When two unbelievers do this, it's meaningless to them.** *They are Godless anyway and couldn't care less,* but when one feels they are God's Child, it's devastating. When I was going through my divorce, I truly believed I was saved, and I was devastated, but at that time, unbeknownst to me, *I was as lost as I could be!* I was truly at the lowest part of my life and the farthest from God, in Word, in conscience, in Truth, and in actions. **I thought I was a born-again believer; what a joke! I bought completely into my own self-deceit.** This Biblical confusion came twenty-five years earlier. It started when I said a *(sinner's prayer)* many times. I walked that aisle and got baptized. I went soul-winning with the Pastor, who I later learned had run off with the assistant pastor's wife. I gave out Bible tracts. I diligently witnessed to many others. I had Jesus' bumper stickers on my car. **While I was a make-believer, I bought into "easy believism." I believed my own lies about being "born again"; I mistook emotion for true conversion. I only know this as a fact because when I was truly born again by God, EVERYTHING changed! The blinders came off my eyes.**

This change for me came two weeks <u>after</u> my legal divorce, which was initiated by my ex-wife, not me. I was always against divorce. *I thought divorce was for others.* I tried through countless tears and reason to make all things right. My ex-wife was as cold as ice. She started a new life with a new man and loved the world's way of thinking. I was awarded custody of our two little girls during our divorce, but I felt it was best to relinquish guardianship, allowing their mom to have custody of them. That was a very, very big mistake! My ex-wife moved four to five hours away and would hinder me from even seeing them *(which was only every other weekend)* because it was inconvenient for her to meet me halfway. There were many times I would travel four to five hours each way just to see them. I would take them to Church. I did not fully understand at that time that the Church was only for Believers, not unbelievers. However, their Salvation meant the world to me. They both went on to get baptized and started frequently visiting an entertainment "church" with their mom, which only drew them further and further from God's Truth. They grew up with a liberal mindset and did not follow God, but followed the world. They are in my prayers each day. The Bible states in Galatians 6:8, "You will reap what you sow"; I have, and still do. *I was a hypocrite pretending through my life that I was more righteous than I truly was; such are all those who buy into "easy-believism."* **Then God made me a Christian. I then matured through studying His Word. I now fully understand I have no righteousness of my own. My righteousness is only found in Jesus Christ alone.**

My deep sorrow and non-ending painful tears were heard by God. God's Providence and His Election Stand**. I believe God won't use anyone meaningfully unless He hurts him or her deeply** *(See Testimony Poem).*

His plan for my life was put into effect on that life-altering, tearful day. The day He Saved my soul. The day I cried a rainstorm of tears with no end in sight. God is Sovereign and knew when and what He was doing and allowing. God knew I would never write the books I have, being where I was. He knew I could not have changed my ex-wife's mind. He knew she would never agree with His Word. **He allowed it, orchestrated it, and even positioned me through everything I went through. He also knew what would cause the best outcome for me, which would glorify Him.** You see, at that time, I could've never looked fourteen years into the future. God removed me from a failing relationship and opened a new door to what I needed – HIM. God allowed my ex-wife to file for divorce, allowed her to have her life. He allowed her heart to grow harder and harder. He allowed that divorce to happen. Then God saved me for Himself, by Himself, two weeks after. **This orchestration of events is a small example of how God can change and control all circumstances.** When we clearly see a *dead-end sign* in our lives, and we see and feel nothing but deep remorse, sorrow, and darkness in our future. God can then reach down and breathe His *Light of Life* into us. This new life is called Salvation; being Born Again. Amen...

God has brought me a long, long way. Early in 1990, I designed and personally built my first home, a five-thousand-square-foot home. It took me eight months to personally build it *hands-on*. I lived there with my then-wife and kids for over twelve years. After my divorce, it had to be sold, sadly. My closest friend at the time was Dan, who let me stay in a small detached house. This house consisted of one room totaling about *(12'x10')* twelve feet by ten feet on a one-hundred-acre property he had owned. I was very, very grateful, and this allowed me to finally become humble. God knew what He was doing. Previously, living in a five-thousand-square-foot home and later moving into a one-hundred-and-twenty-square-foot home were big changes. I studied God's Word for up to 5 hours each day for nearly 3 years. I was also able to listen to over thirty-five sermons each week from BBN *(Bible Broadcasting Network)*, "Moody Radio," and other *Christian Stations.*" Lastly, I was able to read countless Christian books *(some even from false teachers),* all in that small room. **This was my growing stage, which is ongoing. This hunger and fire for God's Truth has never been extinguished, nor could it ever be.**

In the past, I still had commercial real estate that I was trying to sell after my divorce. I didn't have a TV in that small room, and I didn't miss it. Unfortunately, unbeknownst to me, while I was visiting my brother for a couple of weeks, my friend Dan passed away! Sadly, not only did I have no clue of my friend's death, but I also knew nothing of his funeral either. I left countless messages on his cell phone. His brother-in-law finally called me days after the funeral, informing me of Dan's death, and I cried for hours. He simply said Dan had died and that I must move out of that room immediately. They had plans for his land. The call was hard and cold; Dan was my best friend. He died unexpectedly at age forty-five from heart failure. I look forward to seeing him again. He was a True Believer who taught me a great deal; I miss him every day.

Shortly after, I moved into a small hotel. Then, in 2008-2009, the largest financial crisis occurred. The biggest recession of my lifetime came through. I lost the Real Estate and everything I personally owned. I even sold all my gold and guns to survive. I went through hard, hard times of total financial defeat. I started teaching street self-defense and boxing, drawing on the skills and passions I developed in my earlier years. I was trying to financially survive. I was soon homeless, sleeping in my vehicle and on floors here and there. I moved close to where my kids lived, not knowing what God would do. I lived one day at a time, in deep prayer. God then brought an old friend from my past back into my life, who helped me to find places to stay *(floors to sleep on) and* even small *handyman* jobs here and there. This kept me alive and gave me hope. Soon after, another old friend let me stay alone in a huge, unoccupied house for up to one year! Fortunately, this was still in the same town my kids moved to; God was always working in my life. Later, I rented a room in a friend of a friend's home, paying *on a week-by-week basis.*

Thank God, I was slowly getting back on my feet. I was not close to where I was, monetarily or materially, given what I had lost, nor did I care. **I had Jesus, which is all I needed.** Little by little and through much hardship, God was molding and humbling me. I was then doing home improvement work, was soon arrested, and went to jail for not having a contractor's license in that county. While I was there, I witnessed to others. I soon returned to renovating empty houses for clients and sleeping on the floors of those homes at night. I borrowed money and started studying to take the Residential Contractors test, which I passed. God never gave up on me…

There was a story I heard on BBN radio while at my friend Dan's house. It was from Dr. J. Vernon McGee (Bible teacher and pastor, 1980s*).* His sermons are still on the air in over 120 languages and in over 190 countries, as part of the *"Thru the Bible"* series. This story was told this way: Vernon, a kid in elementary school, was asked by a friend to play hooky. Vernon never heard of hooky, so he asked, "What is hooky?" His friend told him, "We would simply drop off our books in our desk and then sneak out of school." His friend went on to say, "And then we can go fishing." They both went fishing instead of school, but neither caught any fish. It was time to go back to school to retrieve their books. Vernon's friend told Vern (he called him Vern), "Be careful not to let anyone see us." They tried to sneak back into the school without being seen, but the principal saw them and yelled, "Wait right there!" Vernon's friend whispers to Vern, "We are both going to get a whooping!" He went on to say, "Once the Principal bends you over his knee, he will start whooping your backside with a wooden paddle. When he starts this whooping move closer to that paddle, so it won't hurt as much."

Vernon later equates that story to make it more Biblical. Vernon says, "When times get hard, life gets tough, through turmoil and chaos move closer and closer to God, so it won't hurt as much." *Once I heard that, a light went off in my head!* It made absolute sense. **The short moral of this story is change the way you look at things, and the things you look at change! Run to God, and if you fall, get back up and run back to God, over and over. This is the Christian life, moving closer to God. The Best way to heal a broken heart is to give God all the pieces.**

I went out to a Christian bookstore and purchased his five-book series *"Thru the Bible,"* a commentary based on Dr. McGee's radio program of the same name. I ended up owning close to a dozen different "Bible Commentaries," by different authors, by the time I had to move out of that 10x12 room. You see, I once had so, so much; then nothing, nothing at all. **Many times, when you're down to nothing, God is up to something.** When God saved me that tearful night, I gained everything and more in Him. This book is not about me, so I will move on to the subject at hand. I just wanted to show you a glimpse of how **God can change everything in the blink of an eye. We all go through hard times,** but if you know Christ and He knows you, that is an everlasting, eternal Gift. Stay strong, keep praying, stay in His Word daily, and keep working hard and moving forward. Change is coming. **He brought the right woman into my life at the right time.** She edifies me and encourages my studies and my writing. I was not ready spiritually, mentally, or financially to have her until God said I was. She is being used by God to help me in countless ways that glorify Him. There is power in prayer: before we met, she was praying for someone like me, and I was praying for someone like her. She is the love of my life. She is a Godsend. Each day we grow closer and closer together. She is also my very, very best friend.

We are also together, growing in a deeper and deeper Biblical understanding of the fullness of Christ daily. I love her so much, like I never believed possible. She is what I was looking for in a woman for fourteen years! She plants countless seeds of Biblical Truths for Christ. She also edits all of my books and designs their covers! We both created a *"Biblical Bible Tract"* and had many copies made, which my wife and I give out. We also furnish them free to those who ask, including Churches. My wife is also currently writing a book of her own entitled *"God's Guide to Better Health!"* Get a copy of that as well! All the Glory goes to our Lord, Jesus! **The responsibility to plant Biblical Seeds, Gospel Seeds, is of course ours; the results are of course God's.**

All things happen for a reason to those who love the Lord. This points again to **Romans 8:28 NASB,** *And we know that God causes all things to work together for good to those who love God, to those who are **called** according to His purpose.* Let's unpack this verse. Once God chooses the moment to save someone *(awaken them from their spiritually dead condition),* that person then belongs to Him. He or she is no longer of the "world". **He or she becomes one of God's Elect. Their Father goes from Satan to God Almighty, through Adoption.** This is ultimately for God's purposes and yours and mine. God saves those from going to Hell, where we all belong, and through His Grace, they undeservingly end up in Heaven, where we don't belong. This is all God's Grace. This transformation is in God's

Hands only. This good may take fourteen years to be seen; other times His Good may only be seen in Heaven. God used the divorce of two unsaved people to wake up one for Him, for His use. Once I was Saved *(Born Again),* **I started to see the vast differences in how I believed wrongly before. When I thought I was saved, I realized that everything I had thought before that day, Biblically, was incorrect.** I also witnessed the vast differences between my ex-wife and me. God exposed much. God knew what He was doing. **I thank God each day for saving me from my wicked self and from a well-deserved Hell.**

He has given me a fresh new start as His Child. That was just a tidbit of my past. I cannot overemphasize how important good communication is. This is such an important aspect while dating and later in marriage. **If one cannot communicate well or confide in the other completely, he or she will resort to friends who will. These friends are themselves single, or lost, or of the same sex.** This places undue stress on those seeking God's counsel, not on this world. There are other times a Christian may confide in a family member who is not a true Believer, which again is meaningless. **Most of the time, asking for advice from someone who does not thoroughly know the Bible or live it yields only worldly and worthless counsel.**

Those are, again, some of the reasons I wrote this book. Couples, married or dating, have nowhere to turn when faced with a certain request from their date or spouse. **Today, many think that sarcastic humor is virtuous; it's not, it's demeaning.** When things in life get really tough, really fast, we need those who can edify us and rebuild us. Those who use the Word of God find hope for restoration with God and their spouse. **Biblical Communication is, in itself, marriage counseling when applied correctly.** When a marriage brings God's Word into its conversation, it is the time when God is heard. **The ignorance of God's Word is what destroys relationships, which should have never gone past their first date!**

Then there's the motto "Be Yourself." This has become Satan's counterfeit! Let's look at **1 Peter 1:14-16 NKJV** *(14) as obedient children, not conforming yourselves to the former lusts, as in your ignorance; (15) but as He who called you is holy, you also be holy in all your conduct, (16) because it is written, "Be holy, for I am holy."* The Apostle Peter is teaching and encouraging Believers to conduct themselves appropriately. Paul explains that it is God who has called each of His Elect to be separated from the world for His Use, not their own use. **God wants His Elect to be Holy** *(set apart for His use)* **and even more than that to be Christ-like.** Let's read **Matthew 5:48 NASB** *Therefore you shall be perfect, as your heavenly Father is perfect.* Here, Jesus is teaching the crowds what it means to follow Him. This runs contrary to all the world's teachings, contrary to what false teachers preach. There are many so-called "Christians" today who say, "Oh well, Jesus did it all, I can do nothing but be me." This kind of garbage talk is from the unconverted heart. **True Believers actually are changed and want to be like their Father, not like the world.**

When one is TRULY BORN AGAIN, he or she is never the same again. **Christians are fundamentally, deeply, and profoundly changed. They hate the world because it's evil.** The Christian hates what God hates and loves what God loves. God hates sin and throws the sinner into Hell. Those who love the Lord fear God as well. Let's turn to **Matthew 10:28 LSB** *Jesus said, "And do not fear those who kill the body but are unable to kill the soul; but rather fear Him who is able to destroy both soul and body in Hell."* It's worth repeating, if your "date" does not fear God, that's a huge Red Flag! Don't walk away, run!

You should NOT be holding secrets from each other; this is not wise and is sinful. There are sins of omission *(sinning by not doing or saying what's right, holding back truth)*. Then there are sins of commission: what God's Word says to do, but we do differently. Then there are things we know to do or say, but we don't; as in not speaking up when wrong is occurring. Hop over to **James 4:17 NASB** *So for one who knows the right thing to do and does not do it, for him it is sin.* This verse applies to all Believers, not calling out error, not telling others of God's Truth. **When you do NOT correct your Brother or Sister in Christ, this is also a sin.** When you do correct him or her Biblically, and this person won't heed correction, he or she is not in Christ. For many, that insight is a wake-up call, exposing who we thought were True Believers. When you realize this; such a person needs the Gospel again. They are not your Brother or Sister in Christ but are still lost in their sin. If someone tells you they're a Christian but votes Democrat, that's an oxymoron! There is no such thing as a Christian/Democrat!

If you are not telling others the Gospel when something in you says to do so, it's a sin. **When you won't expose false teachers and false preachers but allow those you know to be deceived by them, this is a sin.** When you are afraid to offer Biblical Correction, and you know God's Truths are being attacked concerning any issue, it is a sin. Today, there are many false believers. **The real Born Again Believers don't care if your feelings are hurt; they care about God's Truth and what He thinks and if He is offended.** Those who stand up for God's Truths and risk losing family and friends' relationships are the only True Believers. The fake Christians, the ones who hide and duck conversations concerning abortion, gay rights, gay marriage, and even politics. They are the ones who take sides against God's values. Those siding with the world are the ones God calls *lukewarm*. Those are the ones He throws in Hell. This points us to **Revelation 3:16 NASB** *So because you are lukewarm, and neither hot nor cold, I will vomit you out of My mouth.* We see that Jesus is explaining in general terms what He does to those who are not His, those *lukewarm* for Him. **He vomits them into Hell. We should never be "on the fence" or *lukewarm* for Jesus. You either live for Him, or you don't know Him, period.**

When you go against Truth, it's called lying. Today, some call it a "white lie," a "fib," or say, "I don't want to hurt their feelings," or add "false details" or "make up their own *facts.*" **Lying is wrong, open honesty is vital; exposing God's Truths is not open to counsel. They are to be professed and proclaimed. God's Truths are absolute.** Lying to each other is absolutely not acceptable. Trust starts day one. There's right and wrong, there's negative and positive, there's dead or alive; there is no such thing as being both. **Living in sin is not simply walking on thin ice; it's Slam Dancing on it. God will not be mocked.** Galatians 6:7 KJV *"Be not deceived; God is not mocked: for whatsoever a man soweth, that shall he also reap."*

Here is an example of what God did in the Old Testament to liars. Read **Acts 5:1-10 NIV** *(1) Now a man named Ananias, together with his wife Sapphira, also sold a piece of property. (2) With his wife's full knowledge he kept back part of the money for himself, but brought the rest and put it at the apostles' feet.(3) Then Peter said, "Ananias, how is it that Satan has so filled your heart that you have lied to the Holy Spirit and have kept for yourself some of the money you received for the land? (40) Didn't it belong to you before it was sold? And after it was sold, wasn't the money at your disposal? What made you think of doing such a thing? You have not lied just to human beings but to God."(5) When Ananias heard this, he fell down and died. And great fear seized all who heard what had happened. (6) Then some young men came forward, wrapped up his body, and carried him out and buried him.(7) About three hours later his wife came in, not knowing what had happened. (8) Peter asked her, "Tell me, is this the price you and Ananias got for the land?" "Yes," she said, "that is the price."(9) Peter said to her, "How could you conspire to test the Spirit of the Lord? Listen! The feet of the men who buried your husband are at the door, and they will carry you out also."(10) At that moment she fell down at his feet and died...* We see here how God thinks out loud. **He HATES the sin** of lying so much; this is how He handles it without restraint. **They both dropped dead on the spot for lying!** Do you think Heaven awaited them? We also notice how God takes all lying personally. **This is God, who is also Jesus, with the Holy Spirit together; all Three Persons are always in Total Agreement.** If God treated us like this today, sadly, no one would be standing. If you can see how God is totally upset with lying, don't do it. **Find a woman or a man who hates lying as well.**

Test your date before getting married. Test her or his Spirit. Let's go to **1 John 4:1 MSG** *My dear friends don't believe everything you hear. Carefully weigh and examine what people tell you. **Not everyone who talks about God comes from God.** There are a lot of lying preachers loose in the world.* Let's take this verse and examine it. **We are never to blindly believe one knows God simply because he or she says they do!** There were many who said they chose Jesus, and we know that is not Biblical. God chooses all who are to believe; such are His Elect. Ask your date, **"How do you know you are Saved?"** Then listen to their answer to that important question Biblically. He or she would know they had nothing to do with their own Salvation. He or she would understand Hell should be their eternity and rightfully deserved, but because of God's Mercy, and Grace, Heaven is their Home. Those who think they deserve Heaven are the ones you must run from. Ask him or her, what does Luke 9:23 mean to you? **Luke 9:23 NKJV** *Then He said to them all, "If anyone desires to come after Me, let him deny himself, and take up his cross daily, and follow Me.* Jesus is explaining the true cost of Discipleship. **He says those who want Him must want Him daily, and you will suffer greatly. You will lose your family and friends.** Is that YOU?

Most people fall short of true Discipleship because only God can enable one to tolerate family and friends, persistently avoiding them, and then hating them. Yes, that is how distant your old circle of friends and family becomes, and rightfully so. Let's turn to **John 15:19 NKJV:** *If you were of the world, the world would love its own. Yet because you are **not** of the world, but I chose you out of the world, therefore the world hates you.* **Jesus makes it clear: YOU will be hated if you are for real.** Ask him or her, "How do you cope with the hate and distance your family and friends are initiating?" If he or she does not know what you're talking about, he or she is most likely blending in so well with the world that you can't tell them apart! Not good, big Red Flag!

Those who believe they decided on Jesus must be corrected. If they do not take to Biblical Correction, run! Ask him or her **when** WAS the change in you? Ask, what were you like before God Saved you? Ask, HOW were you changed? Listen to their testimony. Again, let's read **2 Timothy 3:16 NASB** *All Scripture is inspired by God and beneficial for teaching, for rebuke, for <u>correction</u>, for training in righteousness;* let's assume you're dating. If your date doesn't believe that the whole Bible was written by God, run! If your date does not want such a correction, run! If your date says no to your Biblical Rebuke, run! If you are already married to a "believer" who won't allow correction through God's Word, he or she would be a "fake Christian." **A True Believer loves rebuke because they want to be obedient to God's Word.** Fake believers dance around questions concerning God's Truths. These **Red Flags** should never be ignored *(refer to*

Chapter: Think Red Flag). **Remember, examine yourself as well as your date; are you a true Christian?**

If you or your date had to do something, or anything, to be saved, you're adding to scripture. That would then be a work's salvation. Salvation is always 100% God and zero % man. Use Biblical discernment and inquire as to what theological lies he or she has bought into? The most important question is "What do you think about God?" If Jesus is not the most important part of his or her life, **run!** Let's look at **1 John 4:6 NASB** *We are from God. The one who knows God listens to us; the one who is not from God does not listen to us. By this we know the spirit of truth and the spirit of error.* The Apostle John teaches how to identify the same Spirit. **If one does not adhere to the Biblical Teachings of God, they belong to Satan. God's Children want to do as the Lord Commands.** Those who are of the world buy into the alluring lies of false teachers. **We are being buried underneath an avalanche of Biblical inadequacies from today's so-called "pastors."** To find Biblical Truth today is like finding a needle in a haystack. Please be very careful who you listen to. **Read and study God's Word daily yourself**; this is how a person learns discernment. We need to be in harmony with God's Truths.

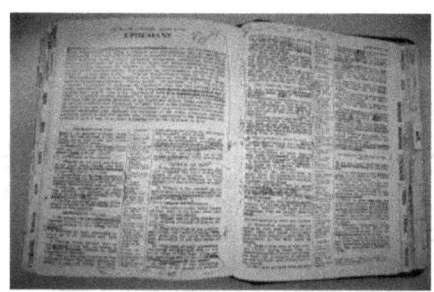

Chapter 11

Save the Marriage

A possible divorce is a tragedy, and if that's what drives you to your knees, you are moving in the right direction. God may be placing you there for His Reasons. This is where a marriage is in dire straits. When someone perceives that their marriage is headed for separation or even divorce, they see no hope of restoration, no trust in each other, and no hope at all. This is a predicament: the above Chapters of this book were not followed, yet God can still use this book to bring newfound clarity. There is an old saying, "Oh, what a tangled web we weave, when first we practice to deceive!" **Honest and correct vetting from the first date is vitally important.** When couples go through marital issues, it's like "Action – Reaction." This cycle continues until one is wise enough to forgive and RUN to God. Hopefully you both do.

First of all, the word "Divorce" should never be thrown around. This word should not even be used in a Christian's vocabulary, not even while joking. **Divorce is never a joking matter.** Some think it is okay to tell their spouse, "I want a divorce, and I won't ever remarry." This is a foolish remark. The word divorce should never be used as a tool to gain leverage over the other. It is a mistake to try to make him or her do as you want, as if you were getting your own way. This attitude is sinful and evil. **It is not to be used as a ploy to create worry, control, or dominance.** Divorce is NOT a word that is used to manipulate the other. **God hates divorce, period;** so, should you both. **Stop listening and paying attention to the voices of**

this world and start listening to the lamp at your feet. Don't attack each other; attack the problem to solve it, and make recompense. **Showing compassion and forgiveness through honesty are Godly virtues. Avoid arguing; continuous, unhealthy, unproductive conflict burdens one's soul.** When the arguing escalates, the man should stop and immediately ask his wife to pray with him, aloud. This would be giving their situation over to God. Then they can resume their conversation calmly. The conversation must include listening attentively and speaking only after the other person has finished speaking.

This is where many who do not study God's Word each day together end up. **Biblical ignorance is never bliss, but blinding.** This is where the love you both had on your wedding day should now be rekindled and remembered. This is where the words you both said on your wedding day **need to resurface.** Remember, Satan can and will sabotage a marriage or a potential marriage because he hates it when two believers glorify God. The only view the world gets to see of Christian Marriages is what such a marriage portrays. **We should always go the extra mile to make our marriages work. This is where this next poem, before it was even published, kept a failing marriage together. Give it a read...**

Love Even Though

While dating be equally yoked...regardless of how attractive, fun, clever, or charming he or she may be, you both must place Christ first, think of time without end...don't pretend...now is the time to move on and go, before, before you love even though...

Before you enter into marriage...pay close attention to what he or she does, rather than what he or she says...avoid marrying someone's "potential." Look for someone who is God's Chosen, a doer of God's Word, not just a hearer of God's Word...Both must give Christ their entire life...before pronounced husband and wife...

Before you say "I Do" pray to Christ together, your love is truly true...obtain Christian pre-marriage counseling too...If Christ is not first in his or her life, don't marry the fool...If Christ is not in you...you're headed for trouble the two of you...But if you marry...it's for life...husband and wife.

Now, Love, even though...one was wrong...yes, weak in the flesh, weak not strong...Re-build that trust in Christ it won't take long...It's not move on and go, it's Love even though...

Love, even though...one is NOT what you thought he or she would be...you're married for life...the vows were for God to hear and see...you vowed, committed to God to be...Love, even though...one let you down...when wisdom was nowhere in his or her actions found...

Love, even though...one argues the fool, for this was the one you picked to marry you...Love, even though...the dishes are not done, the flowers stop coming, the romance is no longer your dance...if he or she asks for forgiveness you must always, always give the chance...no matter the circumstance...Love even though...

Your reason or situation under God, is not better or worse than anyone else's...nor is his or her fall, addiction, vice...fault...or issue...constitute a valid cause for divorce...only a cause to pray...giving that and all such problems sincerely to Christ today...

Love is not performance-based...not at all about what you can take...not always sugar-laced...never in bad taste...never a waste...love is always giving, is unconditional, and forever forgiving...

If one begs for forgiveness or not, for any fall, you must forgive, that's it, that's all...The example is Jesus, who set the call... never act the fool and repay any fall...

God says you must forgive all, yes, all...And never bring up his or her fall any more...at all...as far as the east is to the west...the ones without Christ, never, ever pass this test...you must learn to forgive and display Grace...Remember how to run your life's race...Love even though...

If she falls, he falls, pick her up...pick him up...pick each other up and lift each other up...it's husband and wife against the world, and with Christ you both win, renew your mind through Christ and re-begin...wherever you are, whatever the scar...Love, even though, for a three-strand cord is not easily broken, let God's Words in your hearts be spoken...Unconditional love is unconditional...forgiveness is eternal...Breaking up, not an option, for whatever the reason that reason is never, ever in season...

Forgive like Christ forgives you...don't let the world control your life, your marriage, your decisions, your thoughts...don't handle your life the world's way...drop down to your knees and cry out each day, always seek what God, yes God has in His Holy Bible for you to hear...has to say...

Work it out...for marriage is always a work in progress...don't know, can't grow...God's Word embrace...both don't let go...she hurt you, he hurt you...so.... Yes, so? ... Love even though...now study more and faith will grow...

Love, even though...one wants to fight...Don't...for that knock down drag out fight, won't make things right...Kill each other with kindness and sleep well each night...Love, even though...you were hurt, smack down in the dirt, remember, through Christ that marriage must grow...not go...There's His Grace you must apply...it will get you both by...Christ can change any circumstance...create or bring back true love with romance...and yet another chance...Love, even though...he or she refuses to obey what God has in His Word to say...ending a marriage is only God's Card to play...God's Grace and Mercy are renewed each day, but never a license to sin, do or say...no, it should never be YOUR way...Always think what Christ would do...start today...

Using respect, serving, and submitting to one another God's way...In His Word does say...Move closer to Christ day by day, and if it seems you've been there before...forgive again and again – and study, discerning God's Word more and more...

Love, even though...whoever tumbles and whatever the tumble...it shouldn't matter, restrain yourself...be at all times understanding and humble...

But use that relationships nose-dive to make your marriage more alive...finding out what's wrong...change...to make it strong, lasting forever and ever long...

Place Christ first in your life...whether or not he or she refuses to do so, doesn't matter at all, that's not YOUR call...Do your part...expose Christ, if He's in YOUR heart...Let go of the anger, regrets, worry, resentment, foolishness, and let Almighty God through Christ do His

Godly part...to bring a refreshing change of heart...Now, love even though...

Pray...yes, pray...Christ will mend it, NOT end it, yes, only He can soften a heart, his heart her heart...or both...that's God's part...Pray for love that endures through all hardships... this prayer, don't miss...

So, love even though...For real love is never self-serving, never fails, love is kind, it makes more love grow...Love even though...Stop trying to make him or her the right one...BE...the right one...let God's Love and true kindness forever linger...remember that wedding ring you placed on his or her finger...Dear friend, still looking for an end?

There's always a way out, yes, a real way out, but it's not called divorce; it's called forgiveness...and God's The True Source...Love, Even Though...

1 CORINTHIANS 13:4 NIV *Love is patient, love is kind. It does not envy, it does not boast, it is not proud. It is not rude, it is not self-seeking, it is not easily angered, it keeps no record of wrongs. Love does not delight in evil but rejoices with the truth. It always protects, always trusts, always hopes, always perseveres.*

This poem puts a finger on what to do when one messes up badly. This is when one or both do what they should've done: forgive. **Remember, no relationship continues to "death does one part" without true forgiveness.** This is when the love of God must come forth, front and center. **The couple must sit down and have a calm, honest conversation about what caused their situation; this allows each to speak without interruption, which is very important.** I recommend taking notes and working towards reconciliation and compromise, which would be wise. Let's discuss what could be done to resolve it. What is the best remedy to bring back what you both had, or to improve on what you both had? The poem, *(love even though)* shows the road towards forgiveness and reconciliation. Although few forgive, we must remember how much sin God has forgiven in us. I look at it this way: "Who am I not to forgive?" Yes, this concept kept me in failing relationships because I was dating "make-believers," not true Born Again Believers, thus this book! I was also not married to any of the people I dated, thank God. I was wrong to even date them, again, thus this book. If you are both REAL Believers, with all your strength, work it out. **When going that extra mile, it may certainly be worth it; it's never crowded there...**

If I had married any of the women I dated after I was saved, I would have had to adhere to that poem. I am not saying that one should be a doormat for the other. Of course, there are some instances where divorce may be the only remedy. That option would be the very, very last resort. If you know you made a mistake and sincerely confess it to God, then admit it to your spouse and genuinely promise to God not to do it again. There is room for true forgiveness. **I do not understand why some spouses won't even sit down for such a talk. Those are the ones who are truly heartless and Godless.** They are the ones who are out to seek new relationships, get all they can from you, and move on to greener pastures. Most people fail to understand that if the grass seems greener on the other side, it may be because there is more manure there, so it will require more watering. **Remember, acknowledging your wrongs is not the same as repenting of them. Don't mistake emotion for conversation.**

Judas merely acknowledged his wrongs without repentance. When a person repents of their wrongs, they make a 180° turn and RUN back to Jesus. **If you are both real Christians, work out your disasters with correction. Pay the consequences by making compensations of some kind, which would be mutually satisfying.** There are NEVER reasons to prohibit your spouse from examining your computer, cell phone, purse, or wallet if they want. **There should be no secrets between a husband and wife.** A husband and wife should feel free and confident in the privacy of their home to take off their clothes whenever they want. They should also feel free, confident, and willing to let their guard down. These are the best days of your lives. God wants you both to love each other in countless ways. **Remember, God is ALWAYS Good; life is always hard, don't get the two mixed up!**

A true man or woman of God listens well, then talks and reasons with you. This points to **Isaiah 1:18 NKJV** *"Come now, and let us reason together," Says the Lord," Though your sins are like scarlet, They shall be as white as snow; Though they are red like crimson, They shall be as wool."* When Isaiah says, "Let us reason together," God is telling Judah to examine the case against them. Then make the necessary corrections. Therefore, regarding your marriage, if one were to, in all genuineness, make amends for the situation that led to your spouse's predicament, he or she may be forgiven. God laid out His case against them, much like a spouse who sinned against the other must explain their immorality or mishap. That person or spouse should beg for the other person's mercy, genuinely promising that it will never happen again; then there can be forgiveness and grace. The couple should avoid any courts or judges and reason

143

together, settling out of court. If both are truly Born Again Believers and realize a mistake was made, forgiveness is the only cure, not running to family or friends.

Nevertheless, there are some Biblically ignorant "Christians" who will jump at a chance to divorce the other, grabbing all they can. Starting over with someone else without learning the real cause of their breakup, or wanting to repair it, is complete foolishness. Reconciliation in a marriage that God put together is paramount. If God did not unite it, why are you in it? Thus, this book! This usually indicates that one or both were not genuinely reborn by God, but through their own deceptive "freewill." In that scenario, both are under Satan's influence, not Christ's. Such a divorce holds no significance for God; Satan is your father instead. Truly, it is extremely uncommon for genuine believers to seek a divorce. Most of the time, one wants a divorce, and the other wants reconciliation. It is common that one person has come to his or her senses, and the other is stiff-necked, meaning stubborn. When a spouse doesn't run to God first, seeing a weakness in a marriage means he or she doesn't have God at all. It's important to fully discuss the root of a problem together; filing for divorce quickly is always unwise. This is called a knee-jerk reaction. It starts up all over again, just with different names, but with similar stories and sadder endings. **Many divorces end with couples citing irreconcilable differences. Sure, they do. One or both don't want what God wants.** These differences sound more like they got married for lust, convenience, or money, not genuine, Godly love.

Let's go back to the beginning. God says do not have sex before marriage, did you? When done, it weakens the marriage and proves that one cannot be trusted to do as God wants. It tells God their lust for sex is more important than His Holy Word. God says both must be equally yoked. Are you? This means you both understand God is Sovereign. His ways are the only right ways. God says the man must lead. Is he? Does the man make Godly decisions? Is he in the Word daily? God says place Him first in your relationship or marriage. Are you? Are you both praying together several times a day, out loud? Are you both studying and reading God's Word each day together, taking turns reading out loud? Are you both reading through the whole Bible together each day? Are you both saying "grace," thanking God for each meal in Jesus' name? This is ongoing without end. Are you each praying daily for the Salvation of family, friends, and other people? **If the answers to such simple questions are no, God is NOT involved in that relationship, period. Why would you pretend He is? You, too, are self-deceived like I was…But God…**

It is very important, before taking a man or woman to be your husband or wife in marriage, that you both realize that the vows you take before God promise a lifelong commitment. **Many people entering marriage think they have a way "out"; this is where many marriages are today.** The vow was "till death do us part." It is a vow of permanency; what many hear is "till one of us is untrue." That is a lie from Satan that they buy into.

Divorce is from an unrestrained lust for what one wants. That type of mindset is of the world; do we really

want to be like the world? A Christian Marriage is never an impulsive commitment, but one well-thought-out and joyful in Christ. Here's a poem that says it all.

Did God Orchestrate Your Relationship?

With Christ Jesus in the mix, any God-filled relationship can be fixed...

Do not be unequally yoked with unbelievers, for light has no fellowship with darkness...This point don't miss...

Did God orchestrate your relationship? Many say yes, they're sure...
But when trouble knocks, do they seek God's Cure? Or if married...simply head out their front door...?

146

JOSEPH MALARA

*Did God orchestrate your relationship? Did you both do it
all...or was it God's Call...?*
Did God bring you this girl, this guy...ask yourself why...?
If you've never once prayed together... here's a tip...
God did not orchestrate that relationship...

Is your foundation together strong...built on the love of Christ?
Or foundation wrong...built on the love of one's...vice?
*Does your heart for each other sing...or relationship based
on...one thing?*

Are goals on the same page...life on the same stage...?
Can you talk about all things...?
*For a lack of communication...causes aggravation and
produces misinterpretation...leading to that relationship's
separation...*
*Do you love the inner person...the passion...the romance...the
lust...? Add to that mix...the fear of God...you must both trust...*

*If you're not married...and you're doing it or shacking up...God
will NOT bless you, nor fill your cup...*

Are you together...studying His Word, each day...?
or doing life...your own foolish way...?

*Does this person supply a certain need...a certain want...but is
it God's Wisdom you BOTH hunt? If not...refrain...that
relationship will cause great pain...*
*Don't harden your hearts, give God all parts...be ready to hear
from Him "Go" or hear from Him "No" ...*

147

If your relationship is on-going...but in God's Wisdom...not growing...

If you're doing the right things...for the wrong reasons...
If you're not defending God's Word during all seasons...
Then God is not intertwined...you're not of the same mind...
and that relationship is running blind...

Your relationship can be sanctified, glorified, and amplified if the love for Christ...both don't hide...

If God Orchestrated your relationship, it would be blessed... all three would be magnified...
A true relationship with God would bring forth a new eye-opening foundation of understanding...there'll be no demanding...

Belief with discernment will grow and grow...if it's from God...it will show...

Seek God's Wisdom in the relationship you're in...
Seeking deeper understanding in God's Word...you'll both win...

Don't be single-minded...be God-minded...Give in...

2 Corinthians 6:14 NIV *Do not be yoked together with unbelievers. For what do righteousness and wickedness have in common? Or what fellowship can light have with darkness?*

Chapter 12

Why the Christian Marriage Works

Trials in life can make your marriage bitter or better. **Love should not be a fight, but worth fighting for.** Good Marriages are full of forgiveness while living in God's Word. **TRUE Christian Marriages are those in which both the man and the woman are Born Again.** This is not as simple as reciting someone's prayer, walking an aisle, or asking Jesus into one's heart. **Only God can make a Christian; it's a GOD Thing, it's Supernatural.** *The Christian life is not hard. It is impossible.* You cannot re-birth yourself nor live out the Christian life in your own strength.

You must both sit down and discuss, "What **is** a REAL Christian?" There is no "free will" in Salvation. Again, Salvation is 100% of the Lord and 0% of man. If the man or woman you are dating or plan to marry doesn't understand that simple fact, you both have much more to discuss. The Bible is clear; God Himself chose who He wanted to Save. Let's read again **John 6:44 NASB** *No one can come to Me unless the Father who sent Me draws him; and I will raise him up on the last day.* Jesus, Who is God, is again explaining how Salvation works. The fact is, if you are not saved, God may not be finished with you yet! Cry out to Him and keep crying out. When and if you do become saved, you will know it. There will be no guessing at it. This book will be very helpful in identifying a false Christian. **If you have read this far and realize you are not saved, God is working; keep reading...**

The reason is that no one truly seeks God, not one. That, again, is Romans 3:10. Therefore, Jesus makes this point VERY clear: those who were chosen by His Father will be His when they die. **This way, no one can ever boast or take ANY credit for doing anything toward or for their own Salvation.** Quoting R.C. Sproul, *"Reformed theology does not teach that God brings the ELECT kicking and screaming, against their will, into His Kingdom. It teaches that God so-works in the hearts of the Elect as to make them willing and pleased to come to Christ. They come to Christ because they want to. They want to because God has created in their hearts a desire for Christ."* This book sets out to expose the evidence of this God-given desire that lives in a True Christian's heart, mind, and soul.

The Bible must be taken in its totality. Real Christians do not *"cherry-pick" verses that* appear to go against the rest of scripture; they do not. The fact is, the unconverted mind only sees what it wants and cannot discern True Biblical Meanings. That is how false teachers teach the

Bible. Let's turn to **1 Corinthians 2:14 LB** *But the man who isn't a Christian can't understand and can't accept these thoughts from God, which the Holy Spirit teaches us. They sound foolish to him because only those who have the Holy Spirit within them can understand what the Holy Spirit means. Many others just can't take it in.* I used the *Living Bible* version here, which clearly explains the difficulties those without true Salvation face as they *try* to understand Scripture. **This is why the *lost* twist Scripture to say what they want it to say; it satisfies them. We see that, whether they know it or not, they simply cannot accept or fully acknowledge God's truths.**

Election was all His Choice *(God's),* not ours. My last book, "Digging Deeper into God's Truth Defines a Christian," covers all of that in great detail; it is a must-read. Please consider reading that book as well. **God is God, and we are but dirt. The dirt cannot look upon God and say, "Why have you done this?"** My point in bringing this up again is to help you thoroughly examine your date. If he or she thinks differently from what the Bible clearly teaches, why would you believe he or she is truly saved? **He or she may merely be religious or simply have morals. If one is trying to be a better person, to be good enough for God, or to be Holy, it does NOT make one Holy *(set apart for God's use).*** If I were born and lived in a garage, that would not make me a car. If I go to "church" every day and pray all day, that does not make me a Christian. **When a person is Saved the Bible will reveal this to them. Their actions or inactions will speak volumes. Their *good fruit* will be evident and line-up with scripture, daily.**

Romans 8:29-30 NASB *(29) For those whom He foreknew, He also predestined to become conformed to the image of His Son, so that He would be the firstborn among many brothers and sisters; (30) and these whom He predestined, He also called; and these whom He called, He also justified; and these whom He justified, He also glorified.* Let's unpack these two verses, aka "Golden Chain of Salvation." Here God foreknew, meaning He chose who He wanted for His Own. He chooses His Children to become more and more like His Son each day. **This process is called Sanctification.** This is an ongoing process of self-examination and Biblical Spiritual growth. **This is one of the fruits that identify the True Believer; he or she grows in Biblical Truths more each day.** When one is truly saved by God, their desire is for the Lord. This passion shows up in what he or she says and does each day.

The fruit of a Believer shows up in their diligent study and application of Scripture daily. There is no way to hide the love of God from a True Believer. Each day, he or she learns more about Christ and becomes Christ-like. God Saves each for His Son. He saves them from their sins and His Wrath. This process, called Justification (all sins forgiven), starts at the moment of Salvation. That's when one is Born Again from God. This process is the changing of hearts, the molding of our minds.

The ongoing results of a true conversion will affect every part of one's life. These changes are revealed each day. His Children grow to be more Christ-like daily. **If one is truly Born Again, they are noticeably changed! If one resorts back to their old self or never truly changes, they were never truly**

saved. The *Glorified State* is to come after we die; such is God's Promise to His Elect, to give us new bodies, ***Glorified Bodies.***

Let's look at **Matthew 13:3-9 ESV** *(3) And he told them many things in parables, saying: "A sower went out to sow. (4) And as he sowed, some seeds fell along the path, and the birds came and devoured them. (5) Other seeds fell on rocky ground, where they did not have much soil, and immediately they sprang up, since they had no depth of soil, (6) but when the sun rose they were scorched. And since they had no root, they withered away. (7) Other seeds fell among thorns, and the thorns grew up and choked them. (8) Other seeds fell on good soil and produced grain, some a hundredfold, some sixty, some thirty. (9) He who has ears, let him hear."* Jesus is speaking from a boat to a great multitude gathered together. **This parable more deeply explains real Salvation and what is also meant by false converts.**

Let's look at Jesus explaining what His parable of the soils truly means; it's **Matthew 13:19-23 NIV** *(19) When anyone hears the message about the kingdom and does not understand it, the evil one comes and snatches away what was sown in their heart. This is the seed sown along the path. (20) The seed falling on rocky ground refers to someone who hears the word and at once receives it with joy. (21) But since they have no root, they last only a short time. When trouble or persecution comes because of the word, they quickly fall away. (22) The seed falling among the thorns refers to someone who hears the word, but the worries of this life and the deceitfulness of wealth choke the word, making it unfruitful. (23) But the seed falling on good soil refers to someone who hears the word and* *understands it. This is the one who produces a crop, yielding a hundred, sixty or thirty times what was sown."* **This parable explains how to distinguish the four types of believers through Biblical discernment. This separates TRUE Believers from Un-believers, Make-believers, and Real Deceivers.**

Those who hear the Gospel and reject it are those who are not God's children or are not yet God's children, because such are subject to Satan's intervention. The seed falling on *rocky ground soil* depicts those who hear the Gospel and are immediately on fire for the Lord; they have zeal for God. Unfortunately, such hype is merely false and temporary because it's of them and not of God. **Many repeat a prayer that some "pastor" told them to say. People using their own "free will" to choose God, which is not Biblical; such soil bears only more and more false converts. I was one, but God...** There are no accounts in the Bible to support such nonsense; there is no asking Jesus into one's heart. Those on fire for God don't run to God when trouble comes. They merely seek money or what God can provide them other than God's face; they seek His Hand. There are many false converts who start listening to false teachers and false pastors, even women pastors *(who are ALL false),* to find acceptance. True Biblical concepts are foreign to them, even hostile. The *seed falling on thorny soil* refers to those who put God aside when things get bad, even blame God. The *seed falling on good soil* is for the ears of those God selects. **He opens their minds to understand the Gospel and the Scriptures; such are ONLY God's Elect.** This points us to **Luke 24:45 LSB** *Then He (Jesus) opened their mind to understand the Scriptures.*

154

No one can make a decision towards Salvation. It is all a decision that God made before He created this world, and no one can decide to follow Jesus. His Children can agree to obey Him more and more each day. **Remember, no one can invite Jesus into a heart. He gives New Hearts to His Children without asking for their approval, permission, consent, or knowledge, and in His Time, not yours, if at all.** It takes a great deal of arrogance against God to say that He needs anyone's permission, consent, or approval to save them. Let's move over to **1 John 2:19 NIV** *They went out from us, but they did not really belong to us. For if they had belonged to us, they would have remained with us; but their going showed that none of them belonged to us.* This verse explains that many so-called Christians are not true believers. **There are many that will fall away from God and His Word because they were never saved by God, only betrayed by their own free will, not enlightened by GOD'S WILL.**

Those who profess they were saved because they accepted Jesus are gravely mistaken. Let's go to **John 6:65-66 NKJV** *(65) And He said, "Therefore I have said to you that no one can come to Me unless it has been granted to him by My Father" (66) From that time many of His disciples went back and walked with Him no more.* **Jesus is again explaining Election and most of those who were following Him left. The reason being they were not Saved or Chosen by The Father.** They were moved by their own emotional or personal choice to follow Jesus. **Again, I thought I had been saved for over twenty-five years, and I was lost, too.** At that time, I made a decision based on my personal feelings, not God's. Therefore, I fully understand this verse. **This book was written so you, too,** are able to make such a *Biblical discernment call* in yourself and also in others.

The few *(God's Elect)* can hear a false teacher preach and call him out. They understand a woman can **never** be a pastor. They realize God is Sovereign, not man. They understand the apostolic age is long gone. They don't buy into "free will" towards salvation. **They are sold out for God's Truths not man's false interpretations of it.** Believers seek God's Truth daily and are not afraid to correct others who profess to be Christians, because **most are not. The Elect are small, tiny lights in a world of total darkness. They are the Children who belong to the *God of the Bible.*** You must *scrutinize* your intended spouse in this way. You will soon find out if he or she is a real Christian. You should look for a Christian whose faith is planted in the *good soil* of God by God. We are not looking for a "Christian" whose faith is planted on the rocky soil by his or her "free will." There are also unlearned believers, possibly a person not yet educated in Biblical concepts and God's Truths. When you show and explain *the Doctrines of Grace to him or her using the Bible, and if his or her eyes start to open,* that's a good sign! If they fight Biblical Truths, RUN, they are as lost as I once was. **Remember YOU cannot save him or her, move on...**

You should never enter into ANY relationship thinking YOU can change the other to better understand or accept God's Truths; YOU cannot! They are spiritually **dead** in their sins; that's the lowest anyone can be. Please understand, neither you nor I can raise the spiritually dead, but you can and should pray for them, and plant seeds of Truth...

When you are on a date, talking about God is the most important thing. A quote from Martyn Lloyd Jones, a Protestant minister & Medical Dr., comes to mind. *"A man who knows anything about this intimate fellowship with God cannot stop speaking about it."* I would concur; to know God is to love Him, and one's world centers on Him, not him or herself. When I was younger, I studied *Kung Fu, several martial arts styles, and boxing for over 20 years.* I read all about Bruce Lee. I knew a lot of his moves. I practiced his moves daily. I have seen all of his movies at least three times. I have read countless books about him. I read the book he wrote. **I knew all about Bruce Lee, but I never knew Bruce Lee.** The same analogy applies to Jesus. Many people know all about Jesus. They read some of the Bible. They have read books about Him and His life. They have seen movies of His life. They went to many types of "churches" that preached Who He was and Is! **They know all about Jesus, but they don't know Jesus.** *A True Believer Knows Jesus.* ***Ask your date using this (question and answer segment).***

1) "What is your purpose in life?" and listen to the response.

2) Ask to hear his or her testimony; is it Biblically based, or did he or she contribute something to it?

3) "What are your goals in life?" and listen to the response.

4) If he or she were married before and has kids, ask, "Who is the most important?"

5) "What's the most important attribute when looking for a spouse?"

6) "Whose choice was your Salvation?"

7) "Who do you say Jesus is?"

The Christian must view the dating process as a job he or she is filling, because it ultimately becomes a position in one's heart that lasts forever. The answers to these questions will give you a good point of reference for what to expect when considering a potential spouse. **The purpose of a Christian's life is to glorify God.** We as Believers contributed nothing towards our own Salvation but our personal sin that Christ died for. The Christian's goal is to grow to be more Christ-like each day. If there are questions about children from a previous marriage, the new spouse must come before any children. It's always God, Jesus, man, wife, kids, regardless of circumstances. This is the order God demands from His Children. The most important attributes when looking for a spouse include the three "L's" and passing the Red Flag test! If he or she says it was a good choice he or she made to choose Jesus, **RUN!** Jesus is GOD and is Sovereign. **If such answers do not place Jesus first, run! Again, Christians do not date just to date; we date in search of a Christian husband or wife. Period!**

Once more, before I was truly saved, I thought I already was, but I was not! I went through some of the motions and knew some of the main doctrines. I knew some Christian terminology. **I would have lived my entire life thinking I was Saved, but I was not.** This is how I know what I know, because I once lived as a professing counterfeit Christian myself. I was living more wrong than right, as for God, I did not see the Light.

I was not able to choose God; no one is. I do know of some old friends who went with me to that Pentecostal "church" I attended, and now, some 20 years later, they are still as lost as I was then. **When one is in blindness concerning their own salvation, he or she is not able to understand God's Election.** They are not prepared or able to yield their false Biblical understanding and be corrected, because they are make-believers, not Born Again by God Believers. **I know because I was one.** False converts are not willing or desiring to study God's Word daily. He or she is not able or eager to do as God requires. **There are many so-called "Christians" who are themselves significantly deceived into believing they did something that made them a Christian.** That is just another lie perpetrated by Satan, which of course includes those working for him, such as false teachers, false converts, and false preachers. There is no such thing as converting to Christianity.

God makes a person a Christian, and we simply build on that Faith through constant prayer, hearing the Word of God, and constant Bible study, including its doctrines.

Let's go to Romans **3:10-12** *NASB (10) as it is written: "There is no righteous person, not even one; (11) There is no one who understands, There is no one who seeks out God;(12) They have all turned aside, together they have become corrupt; There is no one who does good, There is not even one."* These three verses fully explain the need for Jesus. There is NOT one person on Earth who is good. There are many who will say that he or she is a good person; compared to whom? **We must compare ourselves to Jesus, and then we all fail.** God goes on to say NO one seeks Him. This means no one seeks the true Biblical God, nor can they. We are all self-centered *(when you look at a photo of you and others, who do you look at first?).* We are all wicked and evil; none is good. This is a true statement that should be embedded in your mind. There is no one who is good but God. Yes, a Christian is saved and righteous by God, yet we are all sinners. **The only good in us who are saved is Jesus, period.**

Let's read **Ephesians 2:8-9 NASB** *(8) For by grace you have been saved through faith; and this is **not of yourselves**, it is the gift of God; (9) not a result of works, so that no one may boast.* This says one is only saved through God's Grace. **God is under NO obligation to give anyone His Grace.** We all deserve God's Judgment and Wrath, which will send us ALL to an eternity in Hell. Fortunately, He selected some before the foundation of the world to be His. The Bible clearly declares that even the Faith that leads to real Salvation is of Him, not oneself.

Many hear the *"External Call"* of Salvation. This can create emotional excitement, but it only results in a false conversion. There is also *"Superficial Faith"* from within us when one hears the Gospel, but this also yields a false conversion. Then there's the real thing called *"Effectual Faith,"* which only comes from God and brings Salvation to His Own. These verses appear more than once in this book because of their depth of meaning, which points to the doctrine of Election.

Matthew 7:23 KJV *And then will I (Jesus) profess unto them, I never knew you: depart from me, ye that work iniquity.* The Gift of Salvation is only given to those Believers who will know Jesus, those who receive Effectual Faith. Christians are justified by this Effectual Faith and NOT BY FAITHFULNESS. Many people are faithful to their *church*, their false religion, and faithful to a *god* of their own making. God knows His Children, including those He will make His. Notice that Salvation is ALL Him, never the doing of anyone else. It says one cannot work or earn Salvation. Those who try to do things to make themselves look good will not succeed. Walking that aisle will not make it, saying that prayer will not make it, or listening to that "preacher." He adds, **"No one can boast, as in NO ONE can take ANY credit!"** Why do you think that's there? If you understand Salvation has NOTHING to do with you or me, then you are now understanding God's Grace. Salvation again is ALWAYS 100% GOD and ZERO% man.

How do we fully understand why a Christian marriage works? It's because there are **TWO Christians involved,** not one! **Therefore, YOU must thoroughly seek, examine, and investigate a person's Salvation**. This is to determine if it's self-induced or God-planted. Thus, to know the answer, one needs to examine their companion and themselves. Let's turn to **2 Corinthians 13:5 KJV:** *Examine yourselves, whether ye be in the faith; prove your own selves. Know ye not your own selves, how that Jesus Christ is in you, except ye be reprobates?* What is Paul saying here to the Corinthian Church? He wants "Christians" to provide themselves with firsthand evidence, not mere hype, that Jesus Christ is in them. Don't just take it for granted that Jesus is in you. **Are you simply pretending to be a "Christian" or not? Are you growing in God's Truths daily or not? Are you able to call out false teachers and spot Biblical heresies? Do you understand the *Doctrines of Grace* or not?** They are "Total Depravity", "Unconditional Election", "Limited Atonement", "Irresistible Grace", and "Perseverance of the Saints." **These are the *Doctrines of Grace.*** A true Believer must understand and sincerely believe each one; all five of them. They are easier to remember using the acronym TULIP.

(1) *Total Depravity* means humans by nature are thoroughly corrupt as a result of this fallen world due to Adam eating the forbidden fruit in the Garden of Eden. Let's look at **Romans 3:10-12 KJV** *As it is written, There is none righteous, no not one. There is none that understandeth, there is none that seeketh after God. They have all gone out of the way, they are together become unprofitable, there is none that doeth good, NO NOT ONE.* Here, Paul is making it very, very clear that not one person is good, not even one.

(2) *Unconditional Election,* let's touch **on Romans 9:15-16 NLT** *For God said to Moses, "I will show mercy to anyone I choose, and I will show compassion to anyone I choose. "So it is God who decides to show mercy. We can neither choose it nor work for it. "* What Paul is saying here is that Salvation is all of God and His Will alone, not any person's will or person's doings, desires, or their good deeds. It's totally due to God's Will, which was determined by Him before He created the World. This will be evident in a changed life for Jesus and by Jesus. God is Sovereign, and we are not God. Salvation is zero percent man and one hundred percent God! Again, 0% man and 100% God, this is extremely important that you comprehend this. Your capacity to understand anything in the Bible is paramount, particularly if you profess to be a Child of God.

(3) *Limited Atonement*, Let's go to **John 10:11,15 KJV** *I am the good shepherd: the good shepherd giveth his life for the sheep...As the Father knoweth me even so I the Father and I lay down my life for the sheep.* Notice that in these two verses, Jesus affirms that He lays down His Life only for the Sheep, not for everyone. *Throughout the Bible, the Sheep symbolically refer to God's People, His Elect.* Let's again look at and dig into **John 6:44 NKJV** *No one can come to Me unless the Father who sent Me draws him; and I will raise him up at the last day.* Jesus, while preaching, overhears many murmuring at Him, doubting what He is saying and His Deity and Divinity. He speaks clearly to them, professing why they cannot believe nor understand Him, why they are doubting Him. It's because they were not His Children, they were not chosen by The Father for The Son. The Greek word *draws* here is "Helko" which means to drag. Again, as we read previously in Romans 3:11, NO ONE WILL SEEK GOD. He has to drag His Children, thank God for such a Loving Father!

(4) *Irresistible Grace*, those that God Predetermined *(Predestined)* Will Be Saved; they will not refuse or reject His Salvation or Grace. Jesus's death on the cross Will Save Everyone It Was Meant To Save, no one else. Let's unpack **Romans 8:30 KJV** *...whom he did predestinate, them he also called and whom he called, them he also justified, and whom he justified, them he also glorified.* Paul is explaining what God has done in a way that we can all understand. God Predestined Us, *(to mark out, to pick)* He Called Us, *(Chose)* then He Justified us *(removed our sin, past, present and future along with its Guilt and Penalty and Proclaimed Us Righteous)* and He also Glorified Us. Paul uses the past tense as if it had happened, which confirms it's inevitable. It's our New Body's Likeness to Christ, which will happen during the Rapture, (1 Thessalonians 4:16-17) get my book, **"Examine The End Times."**

(5) *Perseverance of The Saints*, First go to **Philippians 1:1 KJV** *Paul and Timothy, bond servants of Christ Jesus, To all the Saints in Christ Jesus...* Here, Paul refers to himself and all Believers as Slaves (bond servants), which we are joyfully, and to all Believers as Saints. Saints live forever in the presence of our Lord. Let's unpack **1 John 2:19 KJV** *They went out from us, but they were not of us; for if they had been of us, they would in no doubt have continued with us: but they went out, that they might be made manifest that they were not all of us.* Here, John reveals the Spirit of the Antichrist (those who are *against Christ)*. **The signs of the lost are those who leave the faith, do not want Christ, deny Christ, or lose their passion for Jesus. This reveals the obvious that they were not saved (born again by God), nor were they real followers of Jesus.**

The Doctrines of Grace are briefly explained here, in a condensed form. In my book *"Digging Deeper into God's Truth Defines a Christian,"* these Biblically correct doctrinal principles are explained in greater detail. If you, the person you plan to date or are dating, or the person you plan to marry, are not fully aware of or understand this Biblical doctrine, get that book! **You both must clearly understand the *Doctrines of Grace* before getting married.** They are the **Biblical essentials.**

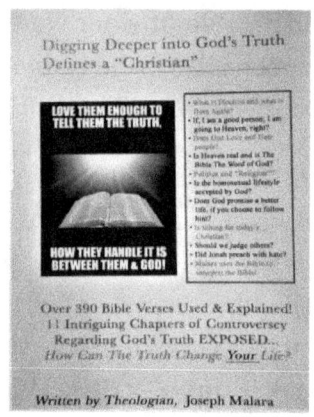

Christians must take care of their bodies. They are The Temple of God! This refers to **1 Corinthians 6:19-20 NKJV** *(19) or do you not know that your body is the temple of the Holy Spirit who is in you, whom you have from God, and you are not your own? (20) For you were bought at a price; therefore glorify God in your body and in your spirit, which are God's.* Paul is writing to Believers. He explains that once a person is Born Again, their body is then God's Temple, and the Holy Spirit lives within us. We were purchased at the highest price ever, the Blood of Jesus the Christ. **It's important to take care of your body as if you will live forever and take care of your soul if you were to die today.** This will paint an accurate picture of how a True Believer should live. **We cannot change God's Truths; we must allow His Truths to change us. Amen... I will briefly explain the FIVE SOLAS.** All True Christians believe fully in the Five Solas. These are five fundamental & foundational principles of the Christian Faith.

1) **Sola Scriptura**, or **"God's Word alone,"** is **2 Timothy 3:15 NKJV,** and that from childhood you have known the Holy

Scriptures, which are able to make you wise for salvation through faith which is in Christ Jesus.

2) **Sola Fide**, or **"Faith alone," it's Hebrews 11:6 NKJV,** But without faith it is impossible to please Him, for he who comes to God must believe that He is, and that He is a rewarder of those who diligently seek Him.

3) **Sola Gratia**, or **"Grace alone,"** it's **Romans 11:6 NKJV,** And if by grace, then it is no longer of works; otherwise grace is no longer grace. But if it is of works, it is no longer grace; otherwise work is no longer work. This is to be read slowly.

4) **Sola Christus**, or **"Christ alone,"** it's **John 5:39 NJKV** You search the Scriptures, for in them you think you have eternal life; and these are they which testify of Me.

5) **Soli Deo Gloria**, or **"To the Glory of God alone," it's 2 Corinthians 13:14 NKJV:** The grace of the Lord Jesus Christ, and the love of God, and the communion of the Holy Spirit be with you all. Amen.

If any "church" adds any "work" to the Five Solas, they would be a lost and spiritually dead "church". These five principles will ground your belief and help you to find the true Christians and Church you desire. Those people or "churches" who tell you they don't agree with the Five Solas or with the Doctrines of Grace are all as lost as I once was. If your marriage does fall to its end, pick yourself up and run to Jesus. If, after a while, you become ready to seek the real Christian relationship you desire, **you must seek God first.** If it's time for you to run or to re-run your Christian race, just keep looking next to you.

The one God has for you will be running the **same race** right up by your side. Keep hope alive and keep thanking God; pray without ceasing. I hope this poem doesn't describe the end of your relationship, even though that's why it was written. **I pray it may just awaken you both to cry out to Him…again…**

If Only

If only we placed God first...then each other...we would have been much more than Christian Sister and Brother...If you would have seen the joy in Truth...and defend it with me...understanding we are the light sent from Thee...His Light...but you never did see...

If only, you would have built me up...not smacked me down, we would've been the talk of the town...many would've seen God in us...then our words a heart could touch...

If only, you would have given in to what God would want...let your man lead...speak softly in love, and plant a seed...

If only, you realized discernment for Truth is worth studying, pursuing, teaching, and doing...and dying in the trying...

If only, you would have studied God's Word each day with your man...no one could of separated us, only The Son of Man...

If only you would have stood strong by your man...nothing is more important than...

If only, you would have stopped living in the past, bringing up every wrong, we could have grown together strong...lasting forever and ever long...

If only, you didn't speak so much of other women, and other men...there would be no comparison then...and our relationship wouldn't have, had to end...

If only, you were teachable...all of God's Truths would have been reachable...together we could of Glorified Him, we both would win...and not given in...to sin...If only we could start again...and you were Born Again...

But time has ended what God never intended...that relationship to ever begin...If only...

Isaiah 55:8-9 NIV *"For my thoughts are not your thoughts, neither are your ways my ways," declares the Lord. "As the heavens are higher than the earth, so are my ways higher than your ways and my thoughts than your thoughts."*

For the Born-Again Believer, Jesus is not simply a token in his or her pocket; Jesus is The Pocket.

Poem Summary

The Poem you are about to read is the true account of my Christian conversion, my testimony. I was alone in pain, crying out to a *"God I thought I knew."* When you read this Poem, you will read about how God opened both my eyes, softened my heart, converted my mind and soul, and awakened me from spiritual death to spiritual life in Him. It happened in the blink of an eye. He had, at that very moment, given me a thirst for His Word and His Truths. The morning after that life-changing night went like this...

The next morning, at the very moment I awoke, I reached out to a Christian friend by phone, while still sitting at my bedside. The first question I asked him was, "How do you study the Bible?" He asked me, "Do you have a Bible Concordance?" My reply to him was, "Whatever that is, I will meet you in 45 minutes at the bookstore to get one," ...the rest is History...

God, I thought I Knew

On my knees desperately broken, crying out loud, out loud to a God I thought I knew, but didn't…

I cried hard "Take my life I have done nothing good with it"…nothing seemed to fit…

I cried and cried endless tears falling down my face, for my family gone, my shame, my guilt, my sin, knowing nothing would be the same, my life totally misplaced, but unbeknownst to me, there was much more I could not see…that would soon, take place…

I cried out "Take my life I have done nothing good with it," as my tears fell like heavy rain, I moaned and suffered with each grieving tear drop, greater and greater pain…

Alone in my anguish, sobbing uncontrollably, crying out loud to a God I thought I knew, but didn't…Unbeknownst to me…

I thought I was reaching out for God to hear me…but He was reaching down to me to be heard…

He said, in a calm, but clear voice of Authority and Power, "Read The Bible…Read My Word."

I clearly unmistakably heard…with my ears, my heart or a spiritual part? In the body or out…only God knows…

As chills rolled up and down my spine…was this all in my mind?

No…I was in deep awe, and today I am still in it…a total surprise…

as my tears immediately stopped flowing from my eyes...my heart skipped a beat, my eyes widened...Who, did I just meet?

I became quiet and still, it was clear to see...His Peace overcame me...I was spiritually dead, until He said, what He said...That night I went to sleep with calm I never ever knew...woke with a Biblical thirst, so miraculously anew...

He Called me...now I do clearly perceive what I could never ever on my own...know, desire, or hunger to believe ...

His plan for me that night, to un-blind me and give me His clear sight...up to then, I lived recklessly through my foolish self-induced misery...crying out to a God I thought I knew...but didn't...Pretending to be a true believer but all the while, a self-deceiver...a make believer...

I am now all His, and His Good News I do tell...His Mercy Saved me from myself...and from an eternal Hell...Although that night, I begged Him to take, take my life...and, He did...

He took my old life and gave me New Life in Him...and took away my sin...I am now Born Again...through Grace by Him. This is my testimony so true...the night I cried out...cried out to a God, I thought I knew...

Ephesians 2:8-9 NKJV *For by grace you have been saved through faith, and that not of yourselves; it is the gift of God, not of works, lest anyone should boast.*

My Closing

In closing, I want to thank you for your interest in these personal yet biblical topics. If this book has helped you in any way, please share it with others so they, too, may be helped. In this book, I focused on the most important factors of a Christian marriage. I included a question-and-answer section. The book explained how to truly identify the True Believer. It also highlighted the importance of real, honest Relationship Communication, saving a damaged marriage, and why the Christian marriage works.

This book exposed what good marital sex is and how it can be even more exciting. If this book helped you better understand what God desires in and from your relationship, then it has done what it was meant to do. If this book brought you closer to God and His Word, it has done what it set out to do. If this book opened your eyes to the ability to now rightly examine another in Christ and yourself, it has done what it set out to do. If this book helps you enter the right relationship with God through Jesus and even grow closer to your current or future spouse, it has accomplished much more than any mere book can. All the glory goes to God... Amen.

My wife's first Book, get a copy!

"God's Guide To Better Health"

You can view video clips of each Book and/or order Books online or at this website

WWW.JOSEPHMALARA.COM

Since the initial publication of this book in 2022, I have authored numerous additional works. All publications and brief videos are accessible on the website, where the books are also available for purchase.

www.JosephMalara.com

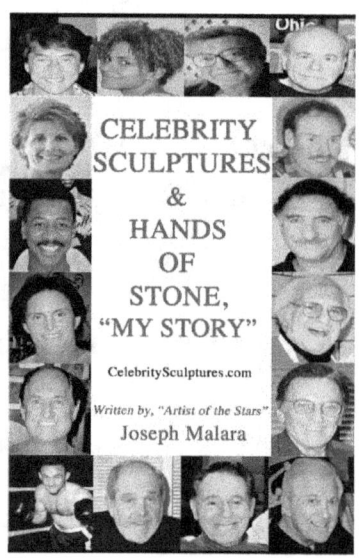

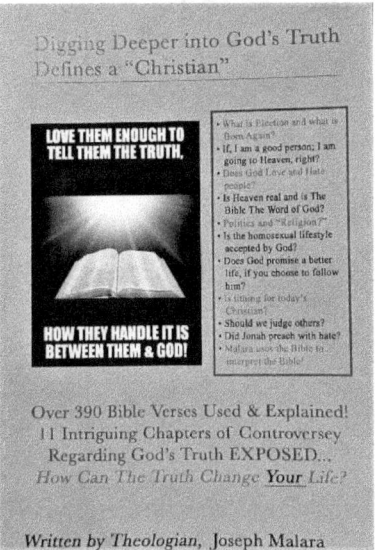

WWW.JOSEPHMALARA.COM

WWW.JOSEPHMALARA.COM

NOTES